The Power of Music

a research synthesis of the impact of actively making music on the intellectual, social and personal development of children and young people

The Power of Music

a research synthesis of the impact of actively making music on the intellectual, social and personal development of children and young people

Professor Susan Hallam, MBE

UCL Institute of Education

University College London

commissioned by the Music Education Council (www.mec.org.uk)

The Power of Music

a research synthesis of the impact of actively making music on the intellectual, social and personal development of children and young people

© 2015 Professor Susan Hallam, MBE

ISBN: 978-1-905351-31-2

Published in Great Britain in 2015
on behalf of the Music Education Council
by the International Music Education Research Centre (iMerc)
Department of Culture, Communication and Media
UCL Institute of Education
University College London
20, Bedford Way
London WC1H 0AL

copy requests
http://copyrequests.imerc.org

British Library Cataloguing-in-Publication Data

A CIP record is available from the British Library

designed and typeset in the United Kingdom by Sonustech Digital Solutions

Contents

Susan Hallam

Executive Summary

The development of electronic media in the latter part of the 20th Century revolutionised access to and use of music in our everyday lives. Music now plays a key role in the lives of most people, particularly adolescents, and is frequently used to manipulate emotions and moods.

Neuroscientific research has demonstrated the way in which the cerebral cortex self-organises in response to external stimuli and the learning activities engaged in by individuals. The brain responds quickly to engagement with musical activities but permanent and substantial reorganisation of brain functioning takes considerable time. The evidence from neuroscience suggests that each individual has a specific 'learning biography' which is reflected in the way the brain processes information. Active engagement with music has a significant impact on brain structure and function. The changes reflect what has been learned and how it has been learned and influence the extent to which developed skills are able to transfer to other activities.

Transfer of learning

The transfer of learning from one domain to another depends on the similarities between the processes involved. Transfer can be near or far and is stronger and more likely to occur if it is near. Low road transfer depends on automated skills and is relatively spontaneous and automatic, while high road transfer requires reflection and conscious processing. Some musical skills (near and low road) are more likely to transfer than others including the perceptual processing of sound, fine motor skills, emotional sensitivity, conceptions of relationships between written materials and sound and memorisation of extended information. Far transfer may occur in relation to the impact of making music on intelligence and attainment, while high road transfer may also occur in relation to self-regulatory and meta-cognitive skills.

Methodological issues

Research exploring the ways in which active engagement with music impacts beyond the development of musical skills has been undertaken within a number of disciplines and paradigms using a wide range of designs and methods. Much of this research cannot demonstrate the direction of causality. Despite this all of the research has the potential to make a contribution to our developing understanding of the nature of transfer of musical expertise to other domains and skills, albeit in different ways. An inclusive research strategy was adopted in accessing the literature for this paper. Academic data bases relevant to neuroscience, psychology, education and music in addition to web-based searches to locate relevant grey literature were searched. Analysis of located documents frequently led to further relevant material.

Aural perception and language skills

There is considerable and compelling evidence that musical training sharpens the brain's early encoding of sound leading to enhanced performance on a range of listening and aural processing skills. Active engagement with music in childhood produces structural changes in the brain which are related to the processing of sound. These changes can develop over quite short periods of time. The quality of aural encoding is related to the amount of musical training and the nature of the requirements of specific instruments.

The enhanced perceptual skills of musicians play a role in the development of language skills. The auditory expertise gained over years of music training fine-tunes the auditory system. Those who have had musical training demonstrate enhanced speech perception on a wide range of different tasks and have advantages in other language related skills.

Early musical training in infants and pre-school children develops the auditory cortex and leads to enhanced discrimination between sounds. There is causal evidence of the role of music training and less formal musical activities in shaping the development of important neural auditory skills. These benefits have been demonstrated with a range of different groups of children.

The development of phonological skills: Active engagement with music plays a major role in developing aural perceptual processing systems which facilitate the encoding and identification of speech sounds and patterns; the earlier the exposure and the greater the length of participation the greater the impact. Transfer of these skills is automatic and there is now accumulating evidence that this contributes not only to language development but also to literacy.

The development of literacy skills

Reading: Phonological awareness is an important precursor to early reading. Word decoding is strongly associated with auditory skills, while reading comprehension requires basic word decoding skills as well as higher-level cognitive processes such as memory and attention. Correlation studies suggest that there are relationships between musical activities and the various skills related to literacy including verbal and auditory working memory. Where research has attempted to demonstrate causality in relation to reading the findings have been mixed. Musical training may have a differential impact on decoding and comprehension.

Research focusing on children experiencing difficulties with reading has generally had positive outcomes. Musical interventions focusing on developing rhythmic skills seem to have the greatest impact.

Where musical activities involve learning to read notation there may be direct transfer to reading text as many underlying principles are similar for the two activities.

While the precise nature of the relationships between musical training and reading skills are currently unclear there is sufficient accruing evidence to suggest that musical training which supports the development of pitch and rhythmic skills supports the development of fluent reading leading to enhanced comprehension.

Spelling: There has been little focus on the impact of active engagement with music on spelling in comparison with reading. Such evidence as there is suggests that musical training can support the development of spelling skills but there is too little research to draw any firm conclusions.

Writing: There have been few studies focusing on the relationships between active engagement with music and writing and the evidence from them is mixed.

Aural and visual memory

Musical training has been found to have long-term positive effects on auditory memory. Children with musical training have significantly better verbal learning and retention abilities. The evidence related to visual memory is mixed. This may be because of the different methods used and the nature of the musical training particularly the extent to which it involves learning to read musical notation.

Spatial reasoning and mathematical performance

Spatial Abilities: The evidence for the impact of active engagement with music on spatial reasoning is compelling. One review of 15 studies found a 'strong and reliable' relationship with differences comparable to one inch in height. The effects seem to be stronger when musical training is early and there is a focus on rhythm.

Mathematical performance: The evidence for the impact of musical activity on mathematics performance is mixed, although there is positive evidence from intervention studies with children particularly where musical concepts are used to support the understanding of fractions. Musical training may support some elements of learning mathematics more than others. Playing an instrument seems to have a greater impact than other activities and the length of engagement and level of commitment are also important.

Intellectual development

Research which has adopted a retrospective approach to studying the relationship between active engagement with music and intelligence has found enhanced performance from musicians on a range of intellectual skills. However, these studies do not address the issue of causality. Those who take up playing musical instruments may have higher IQ scores in the first place, although the evidence regarding this is mixed.

Intervention studies with children have shown that active engagement with music impacts on IQ scores, particularly on elements related to spatial reasoning. If the quality of music tuition is poor and unstructured there is no impact. The evidence suggests that the longer the training the greater the impact and that the relationships between musical training and intelligence remain when a range of confounding variables related to family background are taken into account.

Executive functioning and self-regulation

Executive functioning and self-regulation may act as mediators of the impact of musical engagement on intelligence. Playing a musical instrument, particularly in an ensemble requires many sub-skills associated with executive functioning including sustained attention, goal-directed behaviour and cognitive flexibility. Formal music practice involves cognitive challenge, controlled attention for long periods of time, keeping musical passages in working memory or encoding them into long-term memory and decoding musical scores and translating them into motor programmes.

Evidence from neuroscience research has shown that there are differences in the frontal cortex of musicians and non-musicians, the area of the brain which is implicated in the regulation of attention.

Intervention studies have shown greater improvements in children in music groups in some executive functions as compared with controls.

Participation in formal early music education classes is linked with better self-regulation skills in infants and pre-school children. Intervention studies with older adults support this.

Overall, the jury is still out on the possible impact of music training on executive functions and their relationship with measured intelligence, although it is clear that some elements of executive functioning are enhanced by musical training.

Creativity

Musicians score higher on tests of creativity than non-musicians. Music intervention studies with young children have found enhanced creativity, the greater the engagement with music the stronger the relationship.

The development of creative skills is likely to be particularly dependent on the type of musical engagement. Where the music making is creative e.g. improvisation the effects are likely to be stronger.

General attainment

The evidence from correlation studies suggests that children who experience musical training have advantages across all school subjects except sport even after general intelligence is controlled for. However, the relationship may not be causal as more able children may be more attracted to musical activities.

Evidence from music intervention studies has tended to show enhanced attainment from participants, although there are exceptions.

High quality musical activities seem to affect aspirations which enhance motivation and subsequently attainment. Research with a range of disadvantaged groups supports this.

Music and personality

Personality factors may act as mediators in the transfer of skills. While there are personality differences between musicians playing different instruments many musicians exhibit high levels of conscientiousness. Musicians are also more open to new experiences than others.

Educational motivation and re-engagement of the disaffected

A small number of studies have demonstrated that engagement with music is related to positive attitudes towards school and better attendance.

There is evidence that musical activities can be effective in re-engaging disaffected students including those in the criminal justice system.

Music offers the potential for enhanced self-efficacy, self-esteem and self-concept, improvements in mood, reduced anger, increased motivation and improved behaviour. The impact is in part mediated by the extent that young people have ownership of the music. This varies across contexts and is influenced by a range of factors, including the skills and approaches of those leading projects.

Research with young people not in education, employment or training (NEETs) has indicated that participants' self-confidence and aspirations are enhanced following active engagement with making music. Outcomes include increased motivation to engage in education, employment, or voluntary activity including gaining qualifications, heightened aspirations, and a more positive attitude towards learning. Participants also develop a range of transferable skills.

The context within which such projects operate is important in their success as are the musical genres focused on and the quality of the musical facilitators.

Social cohesion and inclusion

Music offers opportunities for social bonding and cultural coherence. There is growing evidence that musical synchrony creates social cohesion and increased affiliation in infants and adults. Cohesion in classes in schools can be enhanced through extending music making activities leading to better social adjustment and more positive attitudes. These effects seem to be particularly marked for low ability, disaffected pupils.

Group music making has been shown to contribute to feelings of social inclusion; the more frequent the engagement in social musical activities the more socially included children feel.

Music has been used successfully to support the social inclusion of refugee children.

Group music making offers the opportunity to engage in wider cultural experiences, explore new ideas, places and perspectives and support social cohesion through broadening experience.

Participating in group music making may encourage tolerance and the development of social ethics.

Pro-social behaviour and team work

There is evidence of the impact of group music making on pro-social behaviour in children across the age range and adults. Collective music making supports co-operation, pro-social behaviour, belongingness, relationships, collaborative learning, social advancement, group identity, solidarity, taking turns, teamwork and helping others.

Cross community music education projects have been effective in addressing prejudice amongst young people. The specific contexts of each setting can set limits on what can be achieved.

Positive social relationships and the development of trust and respect are crucial for the functioning of small musical groups.

Empathy and emotional intelligence

Participation in active music making may increase the development of empathy and emotional sensitivity in children.

Musicians tend to have higher trait emotional intelligence (a behavioural trait) than others but not ability emotional intelligence (skill in processing emotional information and using it in everyday life).

Psychological well-being

The benefits of active engagement with music in relation to psychological well-being across the lifespan are well documented. Music is increasingly being recognised for its beneficial effects on physical health and wellbeing.

People from a range of different backgrounds can experience benefits to their emotional and physical well-being from making music with an increased sense of self-worth, enhanced social skills and wider social networks.

Babies born premature or underweight can benefit from the stimulation of music reducing inconsolable crying and leading to improvement in physiological measures including heart rate, respiration rate, oxygen saturation and mean arterial pressure.

Music therapy with hospitalized infants has shown robust results in relation to infants' capacity to self-regulate and engage in social interaction. Parent-infant interactions and communication can benefit from joint musical activities.

Research with disadvantaged and disabled children and their parents has demonstrated benefits in terms of parent and child behaviours, parent-reported irritable parenting, educational activities in the home, parent mental health, child communication and social play skills.

Musical activities can lead to a sense of accomplishment, enhanced determination and persistence and of children being better able to cope with anger and express their emotions more effectively. There are also reported benefits in terms of discipline, time management, relaxation, coping with difficulties, communication, and the ability to work with others.

Research with 'looked after children' has shown that engagement in high quality music-making projects can support the development of resilience when dealing with the challenges that they face. Music-making can contribute to improved negotiation skills, co-operative working and learning to trust peers. It also provides respite from problems and opportunities for having fun.

Music making can play a role in supporting the healing of those who have been traumatized. Creative musical activities can benefit children who have experienced war promoting the development of self-esteem, trust and identity.

Personal development and self-beliefs

Active engagement with music can support the development of musical and other identities and impact on self-beliefs. Depending on the nature of feedback received from others these may be positive or negative. Most of the evidence supports the positive impact of music on self-esteem and self-confidence. Opportunities to perform and receive positive feedback are important in this process.

Intervention studies have shown that school-based music classes can prevent a decline in global self-esteem measures.

Most evaluations of programmes for disadvantaged children point to the positive impact on self-beliefs. This is attributed to recognition by participants of their own abilities and these being acknowledged by families and friends.

Group music making can act as a vehicle for change for children with behavioural problems leading to reductions in aggression and improvement in self-esteem. There is also evidence of positive benefits for children with autism and a range of special educational needs.

Music and health

There is increasing interest in the role of music in enhancing health. The impact of music on psychological wellbeing and subsequently good health is largely, although not exclusively, through the emotions it evokes which can be wide ranging.

Music has a particular role in the reduction of stress and anxiety and related to this the reduction of pain and the strengthening of the immune system.

Many health benefits are reported from adult participants in music making. It is likely that these benefits also apply to young people and children.

Music in hospitals has been used effectively to promote the well-being of young patients enhancing relaxation, providing distraction and helping them to cope with their hospital experiences. In some cases music making can reduce or remove the need for sedation.

There are benefits of music making to the families of children in hospital. Parents value being able to participate in musical activities with their child as this enables them to share the hospital experience.

Physical development

There is relatively little research exploring the impact of active engagement with making music on physical development despite the fact that children and adults frequently respond to music with movement.

Neuroscientific research has shown that extensive instrumental music training affects the anatomy of the brain with greater gray matter volumes in motor-related areas.

Using rhythmic accompaniment to support physical education programmes can improve performance.

Learning to play an instrument improves fine motor skills particularly when training commences before the age of seven.

Conclusions

There is accruing evidence which indicates that actively making music can contribute to the enhancement of a range of non-musical skills and lead to other beneficial outcomes.

Research continues to explore the circumstances under which these benefits may occur. A recent review of the evidence from neuroscience suggests that early engagement may be important (before the age of seven), the length of musical engagement and commitment to it, the type of training, and the instrument learned. The quality of teaching is also crucial as to whether any benefits are realised. When teaching is poor there may be no benefits and negative outcomes.

The common characteristics of musical programmes which are beneficial are emerging. They need to be highly interactive and enjoyable with opportunities for: developing new skills and performing; acquiring cultural capital; developing interpersonal bonds and solidarity in pursuing shared goals; on-going intensity and frequency of contact; developing mutual respect; and recognition and rewards for excellence. Receiving positive affirmation from others relating to musical activities, particularly performance is crucial in enhancing self-beliefs whatever the age of the participants. If performances are in high status cultural venues the impact is enhanced.

Implications for education

The research undertaken to date suggests that:

- active engagement with making music should start early for the greatest benefits to be realised;
- engagement needs to be sustained over a long period of time to maximise the benefits;
- the activities need to include group work;
- opportunities need to be available for performance;
- the quality of teaching needs to be high;
- the curriculum needs to be broadly based including activities related to pitch and rhythm, singing, instrumental work, composition and improvisation, and the reading of notation;
- to have a positive impact on disaffected and at-risk young people, the musical activities need to be in a genre with which they can relate.

a research synthesis on the impact of actively making music on the intellectual, social and personal development of children and young people

Introduction

The development of electronic media in the latter part of the 20th century revolutionised access to and use of music in our everyday lives. We can turn on the radio, play a CD, download music from the internet onto an iPod, or listen to music on video or TV with very little effort. This has not always been the case. Prior to these developments, music was only accessible for most people if they made it themselves or attended particular religious or social events. The effect of these changes has been dramatic. It is now possible for individuals to use music to manipulate personal moods, arousal and feelings, and create environments which may manipulate the ways that other people feel and behave. Individuals can and do use music as an aid to relaxation, to overcome powerful emotions, to generate the right mood for social activities, to stimulate concentration, in short, to promote their well being. It has become a tool to be used to enhance self presentation and promote development. Alongside this, technological advances in research techniques have increased understanding of the way that music can benefit the intellectual, social and personal development of children and young people. This paper considers the evidence from that research.

There is extensive evidence of the key role that music plays in people's lives (Sloboda et al., 2009). Music, itself, can generate feelings of wellbeing, can facilitate working through difficult emotions, and is frequently linked to spirituality (Juslin and Sloboda, 2001). It is widely used for exploring and regulating emotions and moods (e.g. Juslin and Laukka, 2004; North et al., 2004; Saarikallio, 2011; Shifriss & Bodner, 2014) and can be effective in inducing positive affective states (North et al., 2004), achieving desirable moods (Vastfjall, 2002) and also for coping with negative moods and emotions (Miranda and Claes, 2009; Shifriss & Bodner, 2014). The most common activity for mood regulation is listening to music (Saarikallio & Erkkila, 2007). Even adolescents who play an instrument report that the best activity for mood regulation is listening to music alone (Saarikallio, 2006).

In adolescence, music makes a major contribution to the development of self-identity. It plays an important role in teenagers' lives (Bonneville-Roussy et al., 2013; Bosacki & O'Neill, 2013; Greasley & Lamont, 2011). Teenagers listen to music to pass time, alleviate boredom, relieve tension, and distract themselves from worries (North et al., 2000; Tarrant et al., 2000; Zillman & Gan, 1997). Music is seen as a source of support when they are feeling troubled or lonely, acting as a mood regulator, helping to maintain a sense of belonging and community (Schwartz & Fouts, 2003; Zillman & Gan, 1997). It is also used in relation to impression management needs. By engaging in social comparisons adolescents are able to portray their own peer groups more positively than other groups in their network and are thus able to sustain positive self-evaluations. Music facilitates this process (Tarrant et al., 2000).

Neuroscience

Recent advances in the study of the brain have enabled us to enhance our understanding of the way that active engagement with music influences other development. Although our knowledge of the way the brain works is still in its infancy some of the fundamental processes involved in learning have been established. The human brain contains approximately 100 billion neurons a considerable proportion of which are active simultaneously. Information processing is undertaken largely through interactions between them, each having approximately a thousand connections with other neurons. When we learn there are changes in the growth of axons and dendrites and the number of synapses connecting neurons, a process known as synaptogenisis. When an event is important enough or is repeated sufficiently often synapses and neurons fire repeatedly indicating that this event is worth remembering (Fields, 2005). In this way changes in the efficacy of existing connections are made. As learning continues and particular activities are engaged with over time myelination takes place. This involves an increase in the coating of the axon of each neuron which improves insulation and makes the established connections more efficient. Pruning also occurs, a process which reduces the number of synaptic connections, enabling fine-tuning of functioning. Through combinations of these processes, which occur over different time scales, the cerebral cortex self-organises in response to external stimuli and the individual's learning activities (Pantev et al., 2003). Extensive active engagement with music induces cortical re-organisation producing functional changes in how the brain processes information. If this occurs early in development the alterations may become hard-wired and produce permanent changes in the way information is processed (e.g. Schlaug et al., 1995a; 1995b).

The brain responds relatively quickly to new activities. Bangert and colleagues (2001) showed through a topographical analysis of very low event-related potentials (ERPs) that audio-motor coupling occurred following a 20 minute piano lesson. Lappe and colleagues (2008) reported ERP changes in young adults after two weeks of music training and Moreno and Besson (2006, Moreno et al., 2009) showed brain plasticity effects on language after a short time actively engaging with music. Playing a musical instrument also seems to speed up brain maturation. For instance, Hudziak and colleagues (2014) found more rapid cortical thickness maturation within areas implicated in motor planning and coordination, visuospatial ability, and emotion and impulse regulation following musical training.

Permanent and substantial reorganisation of brain functioning takes considerable time. Long years of active engagement with particular musical activities in Western classical musicians are associated with an increase in neuronal representation specific for the processing of the tones of the musical scale, the largest cortical representations being found in musicians playing instruments for the longest periods of time (Pantev et al., 2003). Changes are also specific to the particular musical activity undertaken (Munte et al., 2003). Functional auditory responses are greatest in the areas of the musician's own instrument demonstrating timbral specificity to their training background (Pantev et al., 2001). Processing of pitch in string players is characterised by longer surveillance and more frontally distributed event-related brain potentials attention. Drummers generate more complex memory traces of the temporal organisation of musical sequences and conductors demonstrate greater surveillance of auditory space (Munte et al., 2003). Compared with non-musicians, string players have greater somatosensory representations of finger activity, the amount of increase depending on the age of starting to play (Pantev et al., 2003). Pianists, violinists and non-musicians are differentiated by the morphology of the motor cortex (Bangert & Schlaug, 2006), while trumpet players have greater functional activation in the cerebellum, the dominant sensorimotor cortex and the left auditory cortex than pianists (Gebel et al., 2013).

Clearly, the brain develops in very specific ways in response to particular learning activities and the extent of change depends on the length of time engaged with learning. The ways that we learn are also reflected in specific brain activity. When students (aged 13-15) were taught to judge symmetrically structured musical phrases as balanced or unbalanced using traditional instructions about the differences (including verbal explanations, visual aids, notation, verbal rules, playing of musical examples), or participating in musical experiences (singing, playing, improvising or performing examples from the musical literature), activity in different brain areas was observed (Altenmuller et al., 1997). Tervaniemi and colleagues (2001) have also suggested that musicians who play by ear and improvise may learn to process complex musical information more accurately than classically trained musician with corresponding differences in auditory neural responses. The tools and practices utilised to support the acquisition of particular musical skills have a direct influence on brain development and preferred approaches to undertaking musical tasks, also influencing approaches to tasks outside music. Musicians with similar observable skills may have developed different approaches to developing them which may or may not facilitate transfer to other tasks.

Overall, the evidence from neuroscience suggests that each individual has a specific 'learning biography' which is reflected in the way the brain processes information (Altenmuller, 2003:349). Active engagement with music has a significant impact on brain structure and function (Merrett et al., 2013; Norton et al., 2005). As individuals engage with different musical activities over long periods of time permanent changes occur in the brain. These changes reflect what has been learned and how it has been learned. They also influence the extent to which developed skills are able to transfer to other activities.

Susan Hallam

Transfer of learning

The transfer of learning from one domain to another depends on similarities between the processes involved. Transfer between tasks is a function of the degree to which the tasks share cognitive processes. Transfer can be near or far and is stronger and more likely to occur if it is near. Salomon and Perkins (1989) also refer to low and high road transfer. Low road transfer depends on automated skills and is relatively spontaneous and automatic, for instance, in the case of processing of music and language, using the same skills to read different pieces of music or text. High road transfer requires reflection and conscious processing, for instance, adopting similar skills in solving different kinds of problems.

Some musical skills (near and low road) are more likely to transfer than others, for instance, those relating to the perceptual processing of sound (timing, pitch, timbre and rule governed grouping information), fine motor skills, emotional sensitivity, conceptions of relationships between written materials and sound (reading music and text), and memorisation of extended information (music and text) (Norton et al., 2005; Schellenberg, 2003). Far transfer may occur in relation to the impact of making music on intelligence and attainment. High road transfer may also occur in relation to the skills acquired through learning to play a musical instrument, for instance, being able to recognise personal strengths and weaknesses, being aware of a range of possible strategies (task related and personal relating to motivation, concentration), monitoring progress and evaluating outcomes.

The aim of this paper is to consider what we know about the ways that transfer can occur in relation to the skills developed through active engagement with music and how they may impact on intellectual, social and personal skills. The paper synthesises indicative research findings and considers the implications for education.

Susan Hallam

Methodological issues

Research exploring the ways in which active engagement with music impacts beyond the development of musical skills has been undertaken within a number of disciplines and paradigms. The designs and methods adopted vary widely as do the sizes of the samples of participants. Much early research considering the impact of engaging with music on other skills was based on correlation studies undertaken with professional or young musicians with varying levels of expertise. Some research has made comparisons between groups identified as musicians or non-musicians. This research has been and continues to be useful in high-lighting areas of possible transfer. What it is unable to do is identify the direction of causality, although studies using multiple regression analyses are able to take into account many possible confounding factors. Experimental studies where the outcomes of musical interventions are compared with those where there is no musical intervention offer the possibility of establishing causality. Such studies vary in the length of the intervention, the range of measures adopted to measure outcomes and the ages of the participants. This can produce conflicting evidence. Qualitative research (interviews, focus groups, ethnographic and case studies) is able to provide insights into the perceptions of participants and the contexts within which music may have a wider impact. All of this research has the potential to make a contribution to our developing understanding of the nature of transfer of musical expertise to other domains and skills albeit in different ways. An inclusive research strategy was adopted in accessing the literature for this paper. Academic data bases relevant to neuroscience, psychology, education and music in addition to web-based searches to locate relevant grey literature were searched. Analysis of located documents frequently led to further relevant material. The following sections will synthesise the findings from a wide range of studies to further develop our understanding of whether the skills gained through actively participating in making music can transfer and if so what circumstances might support this.

Susan Hallam

Aural perception and language skills

When we listen to music or speech we process an enormous amount of information rapidly without our conscious awareness (Blakemore & Frith, 2000). The ease with which we and other animals do this depends on prior sound experiences (e.g. Krishnan et al., 2005; Krizman et al., 2012; White-Schwoch et al., 2013). This knowledge is implicit, learned through exposure to particular environments, and is applied automatically whenever we listen to music or speech (Bigand & Poulin-Carronnat, 2006). It is therefore not surprising that musical training sharpens the brain's early encoding of sound leading to enhanced performance on a range of listening skills (Hyde et al., 2009; Pantev et al., 2001; Patel & Iverson, 2007; Tallal & Gaab, 2006) improving the ability to distinguish between rapidly changing sounds (Gaab et al., 2005) and enhancing auditory discrimination (Schlaug et al., 2005) thus having an impact on the cortical processing of linguistic pitch patterns (Magne et al., 2006; Schon et al., 2004). There is now considerable accumulated evidence that active engagement with music in childhood produces structural changes in the brain which are related to the processing of sound (e.g. Elbert et al., 1995; Hutchinson et al., 2003; Pantev et al., 2001; 2003; Pascual-Leone, 2001; Schlaug et al., 1995a; 1995b). The evidence also suggests that the influence of musical training emerges quickly. For instance, eight year old children with just eight weeks of musical training differed from controls in cortical event related potentials (ERPs) (Moreno & Besson, 2006), while training for 25 minutes over a seven week period led to changes in electroencephalogram (EEG) frequencies associated with enhanced cognitive processing (Flohr et al., 2000).

Some research has focused on making comparisons between sound processing in musicians and non musicians. This has demonstrated that musicians have enhanced abilities to process pitch and temporal sound information (Kishon-Rabin et al., 2001; Micheyl et al., 2006; Parberry-Clark et al., 2011; Strait et al., 2010). At the sub-cortical level musicians demonstrate more robust and quicker auditory brainstem responses to music (Lee et al., 2009; Musacchia et al., 2007) and speech (Bidelman et al., 2009; Bidelman & Krishnan 2010; Musacchia et al., 2007; Parberry-Clark et al, 2009a; 2009b; Wong et al., 2007). The extent of subcortical consonant discrimination in noise perception is also enhanced in musicians (Parberry-Clark et al., 2012). They exhibit enhanced cortical evoked potentials to deviations in pitch and meter (Chobert et al, 2011; 2014;

Marie et al, 2011a; 2011b; Marques et al, 2007; Tervaniemi et al, 1997; van Zuijen et al., 2005) and have been shown to demonstrate greater perceptual acuity of rapid spectro-temporal changes (Gaab et al., 2005) and harmonic differences (Corrigall and Trainor, 2009; Musacchia et al., 2008; Zendel & Alain, 2009), as well as greater neural representation of harmonics (Koelsch et al., 1999; Lee et al., 2009; Musacchia et al., 2008; Parbery-Clark et al., 2009a; Shahin et al., 2005; Zendel & Alain, 2009). They also have enhanced neural capacity for the perception and processing of vocally expressed emotion (Strait et al., 2009a, 2009b) and have high-functioning peripheral auditory systems.

The quality of aural encoding is related to the amount of musical training (Wong et al., 2007) and also the nature of instrumental requirements. Rauscher and Hinton (2011) using four discrimination tasks with adults aged 16-63, musicians and non-musicians, found that auditory discrimination was better in the musicians, particularly the string players as compared with percussionists probably as a consequence of the many years of subtle tonal discrimination required to play a stringed instrument. The findings demonstrated that expertise in playing a musical instrument selectively improved discrimination thresholds corresponding to the skills emphasised by training in that instrument.

The enhanced perceptual skills of musicians play a role in the development of language skills (Gaab et al., 2005, Jakobsob et al., 2003; Tallal & Gaab 2006). Strait and Kraus (2011a; 2011b) argued that the auditory expertise gained over years of music training fine-tunes the auditory system strengthening the neurobiological and cognitive underpinnings of speech and music processing including enhancing neural responses to changes in pitch, duration, intensity and voice onset time (e.g. Chobert et al., 2011; Jentschke & Koelsch, 2009; Marie et al., 2011a; 2011b; Magne et al., 2006; Schon et al, 2004;). Those who have had musical training demonstrate enhanced speech perception on a wide range of different tasks. For instance, they can perceive speech better than those without training when it is accompanied by noise (Parbery-Clark et al., 2009a; 2009b; 2011), can identify syllables presented when spectral information is degraded (Elmer et al., 2012), identify whether sentences in a foreign language which is tone based are the same or different (Marie et al., 2011a; 2011b) and predict the ability to perceive and produce subtle phonetic contrasts in a second language (Slevc & Miyake, 2006). They also perform better than untrained individuals on measures of language abilities other than speech perception. For instance, they exhibit advantages at making judgments about grammar (Patston & Tippett, 2011), are better at correctly pronouncing irregularly spelled words (Jakobson et al., 2008; Stoesz et al., 2007), remembering lyrics (Kilgour et al., 2000) and short excerpts of speech (Cohen et al., 2011), have a larger vocabulary (Forgeard et al., 2008) and in one study showed enhanced comprehension of complicated passages of text (Thompson et al., 2012).

In addition to the comparisons between adult musicians and non-musicians, a number of studies have focused on the development of musical skills and auditory discrimination in young children. For instance, Trainor and colleagues (2003) found that four year olds who had received Suzuki training had a better developed auditory cortex and were able to discriminate better between sounds. Fujioka and colleagues (2006) recorded auditory evoked responses to a violin tone and a noise-burst stimulus in 4- to 6-year-old children in four repeated measurements over a one-year period using magneto encephalography. Half of the children had participated in music lessons throughout the year while the others had had no music lessons. A clear musical training effect was found in response to the violin stimuli. Shahin and colleagues (2004) measured auditory evoked potentials (AEPs) in response to piano, violin, and pure tones twice in a group of 4- to 5-year-old children enrolled in Suzuki music lessons and in non-musician controls. Where children were learning to play an instrument (piano or violin) AEPs observed for the instrument played were comparable to those of non-musician children approximately three years older in chronological age suggesting that the neocortical synaptic matrix is shaped by an accumulation of specific auditory experiences and that this process is accelerated in those who have musical training. The children playing the piano also exhibited increased power of induced timbre-specific gamma band activity for piano tones with one year of training in comparison with controls (Shahin et al., 2008). In a study with children aged 2-3 years old, Putkinen and colleagues (2013) found a relationship between informal musical activities with parents at home and auditory event-related potentials linked to sound discrimination and attention. They showed that children with higher levels of musical activity had heightened sensitivity to temporal acoustic changes, more mature auditory change detection, and less distractibility suggesting that informal musical experiences enhance the development of auditory abilities in early childhood. Additionally children in the research who attended a music play school until the age of 4 or 6 displayed more rapid development of neural responses than those who gave up the activity. Taken together these studies provide causal evidence of the role of music training and less formal musical activities in shaping the development of important neural auditory skills.

Some recent research has focused on children who have been perceived as at-risk because of their deprived backgrounds. Kraus and colleagues (2014) used a randomised control trial to investigate whether community music participation could induce a change in auditory processing in children with deprived backgrounds. The programme provided free music instruction to the children who were considered as at-risk for learning and social problems. Forty-four children aged 80 to 112 months living in gang reduction zones in Los Angeles participated. The children were randomly assigned to participate or defer musical participation for one year. The children who completed two years of music training had a stronger neurophysiological distinction of stop consonants and neural mechanisms linked to reading and language skills. One year of training was sufficient to elicit changes in nervous system functions. Greater amounts of instrumental music training were associated with larger gains in neural processing.

Another strand of research has focused on school aged children where music has long been argued to provide effective experiences for children to develop listening skills and to support children with learning difficulties (Hirt-Mannheimer, 1995; Humpal & Wolf, 2007; Wolf, 1992). This has been supported by neuroscientific research. For instance, Moreno and colleagues (2009) conducted a longitudinal study with 32 eight year old children over nine months recording event-related brain potentials while they performed tasks testing pitch processing in music and speech. The children were pseudo randomly assigned to music or to painting training for 6 months and were tested again after training using the same tests. After musical (but not painting) training, children showed enhanced reading and pitch discrimination abilities in speech. Six months of musical training influenced the development of neural processes as reflected in specific patterns of brain waves and demonstrated brain plasticity in showing that relatively short periods of musical training had strong consequences on function and in increased sensitivity to linguistic pitch processing (Moreno et al., 2009). Similarly, Putkinen and colleagues (2014) conducted a longitudinal study of more than 120 school aged children and showed that children who received formal musical training displayed enhanced development in responses related to pre-attentive neural sound discrimination and auditory attention. No evidence for pre-training in response amplitudes between musically trained and non-trained children was found. The musically trained children also showed superior performance in tests of executive functions. These studies provide causal evidence of the role of music training and less formal musical activities in shaping the development of important neural auditory skills.

Another recent study explored the encoding of speech in quiet and noisy backgrounds in musically trained and non-trained children (Strait et al., 2012). Thirty-one children with normal hearing between the ages of 7-13 participated. Those classified as musicians had been receiving private instrumental training at least since the age of five and had consistently practised for at least four years. The musically trained children outperformed non-musicians on speech in noise perception overall and demonstrated less auditory brainstem response degradation with the addition of background noise compared to non-musicians. Perceptual (speech in noise) and cognitive (auditory working memory, attention) performance correlated with the extent of the musicians' musical training.

The development of phonological skills

The auditory analysis skills used in language processing (phonological distinctions, blending and segmentation of sounds) are similar to the skills necessary for the perception of rhythmic (Lamb & Gregory 1993; Lipscomb et al., 2008), harmonic and melodic discrimination (Anvari et al., 2002; Barwick et al., 1989; Lamb & Gregory, 1993). A number of studies have specifically explored the relationship between phonological awareness and musical ability. Positive relationships have been found in pre-schoolers and kindergarteners (Anvari et al., 2002; Peynircioğlu et al., 2002), in childhood (Lamb & Gregory, 1993; Milovanov et al., 2008; Milovanov & Tervaniemi, 2011) and in adults predicting the ability to perceive and produce subtle phonetic contrasts in a second language (Slevc & Miyake, 2006). Cross sectional studies have shown that preschool and school aged children and adults with musical experience are able to make stronger distinctions between speech syllables than nonmusic students (Kraus & Nicol, 2014; Parberry-Clark et al., 2012; Strait & Kraus, 2014; Zuk et al., 2013). Children with four years of music lessons, aged nine have been found to be more accurate and faster in accurately discriminating syllables that vary in duration and frequency than those not having lessons (Chobert et al., 2011). Having musical skills also enhances the ability to interpret affective speech rhythms (Thompson et al., 2004) and eight year olds with musical training outperform those with no training on music and language tasks (Magne et al., 2006). One study explored phonological processing including auditory word discrimination, syllable segmentation and a comprehensive test of phonological processing in individuals who were classed as 'tune deaf' in comparison with controls. Poor musical performance was associated with deficits in processing speech sounds (Jones et al., 2009).

There have been a number of studies which have attempted to demonstrate causality, i.e. that actively making music enhances speech perception. Gromko (2005) studied kindergarten children who received four months of music instruction for 30 minutes once per week. The instruction included active music-making with movement emphasising a steady beat, rhythm and pitch as well as the association of sounds with symbols. The children who received the music instruction showed significantly greater gains in phonemic awareness when compared to the control group. Learning to discriminate differences between tonal and rhythmic patterns and to associate their perceptions with visual symbols seemed to transfer to improved phonemic awareness. Degé and Schwarzer (2011) showed that kindergarteners who were assigned randomly to intensive training in music, for 10 minutes each day, for five days each week over a twenty week period showed improvements in phonological awareness that were identical to changes in other children who received lessons in perceiving and segmenting speech sounds. A control group who received sports training showed no improvement. Similarly, François and colleagues (2013) assigned children, matched in terms of cognitive abilities, sex, age, grade at school and socio-economic status to music or painting lessons for a two year period. Before the start of the study the two groups of children performed similarly on a test where they had to identify whether three-syllable nonsense words were presented as part of a five minute presentation of a string of syllables. After one year of training the music group performed better than the painting group with the difference increasing over the two year period.

In a series of studies, Rauscher and colleagues (Rauscher, 2009; Rauscher and Hinton, 2011) explored whether children receiving Suzuki violin instruction performed better on phonemic awareness tasks than control groups who had swimming or no additional lessons. Seventy-five musically naive five year olds participated. Lessons were provided for 45 minutes per week for 16 weeks. Prior to instruction there were no differences in the children's performance on the Predictive Assessment of Reading test. Following the intervention the violin group scored significantly higher on letter word calling and phonemic awareness than the other groups.

Further evidence for the benefits of musical training on language comes from Yang and colleagues (2014) who examined whether children's experience of music training related to language skills in Chinese (their first language), English (their second language) and their performance on a musical achievement test. Seventy-seven children who had received formal musical training out of school beginning in semester three were categorised as musicians, the remaining 173 children were classed as non-musicians. Unsurprisingly, the children's musical skills over the 11 semesters of the study improved when they received training but the children's performance in their second language (English) was also enhanced although this was not the case in relation to their first language.

Taken together, there is now a substantial body of evidence which suggests that engagement with music plays a major role in developing aural perceptual processing systems which facilitate the encoding and identification of speech sounds and patterns; the earlier the exposure to active music participation and the greater the length of participation the greater the impact. Transfer of these skills is automatic and there is now accumulating evidence that this contributes not only to language development but also to literacy.

The development of literacy skills

Reading

A wide range of research has been undertaken in relation to the impact of musical training on reading skills. Some of this has focused on whether pitch or rhythm discrimination is related to reading performance in normal and dyslexic readers. The evidence for an association between music training, musical skills and reading skills is typically explained by near transfer theories. Phonological awareness is an important precursor to early reading (e.g. Bradley & Bryant, 1983) and word decoding is strongly associated with auditory skills (Ahissar et al., 2000), while comprehension requires basic word decoding skills as well as higher-level cognitive processes such as memory and attention (e.g. Sesma et al., 2009).

Correlation studies suggest that there are relationships between musical skills and various skills related to literacy including verbal and auditory working memory (Roden et al., 2014a; 2014b). These have been shown to benefit from musical training. Studies with pre-school children, aged 4-5, have found relationships between musical skills, phonological awareness and reading development (Anvari et al., 2002). Moderate relationships have also been found between tonal memory and reading age (Barwick et al., 1989), while length of musical training is correlated with tonal perception and reading age in 6-9 year-old children (Corrigall & Trainor, 2011). The magnitude of the neural response to speech harmonics also correlates with reading ability (Banai et al., 2009). Register (2001, 2004) in music therapy efficacy studies with young children linked purposeful active music participation in early childhood with emergent literacy, reading and writing skills, while Schellenberg (2006) found that length of music training predicted academic attainment including measures of reading even after controlling for intelligence. A meta-analysis conducted by Butzlaff (2000) of 24 correlation studies showed that musical training was strongly associated with better reading scores.

Where research has attempted to demonstrate causality the findings have been mixed. Arts enriched programmes that include music have demonstrated improvements in school readiness in relation to receptive vocabulary (Brown et al., 2010) and literacy (Phillips et al., 2010) when compared to non arts programmes. In a school based Arts programme, which included music, Gardiner and colleagues (1996) showed that children with a lower score on literacy at baseline achieved similar scores on reading tests after one year of visual arts and music training as compared to controls. Elliot and Mikulas (2014) investigated the effectiveness of an integrated music curriculum within a preschool setting on language and literacy skills in a year long study which employed a pre-post treatment-control group design. Students in the treatment group received instruction using an integrated music curriculum as part of their preschool instruction. The findings showed that the students in the treatment group showed significantly greater gains in language and literacy with an effect size of .24.

Welch and colleagues (2012) evaluated the impact of a music programme which linked literacy activities with a range of musical activities including chanting, clapping, copying and composing rhythms and improvising using rhymes and alliterative or unusual vocabulary. Children participating in the musical activities showed on average 8.4 months of reading improvement compared with 1.8 months for the controls. However, a meta-analysis of six experimental studies (Butzlaff, 2000) which varied in the type of musical training and the reading tests used found no causal effects. In contrast, a later meta-analysis (Standley, 2008) of 30 experimental studies that examined the effect of music intervention on prereading and word decoding skill found a strong overall effect.

An early study where music instruction was specifically designed to develop auditory, visual and motor skills in 7-8 year old students over a period of 6 months, found that the mean reading comprehension scores of the intervention group increased while those of the control group did not (Douglas & Willatts, 1994). Good and colleagues (2002) worked with kindergarten children who participated in a weekly music intervention lasting 30 minutes which consisted of singing, body percussion activity, movement, instrument playing, singing and the use of graphic notation. On completion of the programme the music group exhibited significantly higher phoneme-segmentation fluency as compared with controls. In a study of 8-year-olds who were assigned pseudo-randomly to six months of music or painting tuition, the children in the music group showed larger pre- to post-test improvement in reading irregularly spelled words (Moreno et al., 2009). In a follow-up study with pseudo-random assignment of 4- to 6-year-olds to 4 weeks of daily, computer-controlled lessons in music listening or visual arts, children in the music group had larger pre- to post-test increases in vocabulary (Moreno et al., 2011a, 2011b). The music group also showed greater improvement on a task that required them to match arbitrary symbols with words, a skill that is a prerequisite for learning to read (Moreno et al., 2011b).

Some studies have found no impact of musical training on literacy (e.g. Bowles, 2003; Kemmerer, 2003; Lu, 1986; Montgomery, 1997). Establishing the main and subsidiary beats in a musical selection has not been found to be a significant predictor of reading in third and fourth grade students (Chamberlain, 2003) and Hartas (2011) found no relationship between parent-reported frequency of singing songs and rhymes or playing music at three years and teacher rated performance on literacy. The strongest relationships were found between family income, maternal education and children's outcomes. Piro and Ortiz (2009) focused on the way that learning the piano might impact on the development of vocabulary and verbal sequencing in second grade children. Forty-six children who had studied piano for three consecutive years participated with 57 children acting as controls. At the end of the study, the music learning group had significantly better vocabulary and verbal sequencing scores. However, they had already been playing the piano for two years with no initial differences in reading between their skills and those of the control group. The authors suggested a number of reasons for this: because it takes a long time for effects to be felt; because the age of tuition is important; or because summer holidays prior to testing may have lowered initial scores. There may also have been changes in the nature of the tuition and the development of fluency in reading music which impacted on transfer.

Reading requires the development of both decoding and comprehension skills. Decoding skills are a prerequisite for being able to comprehend. Musical training may have a differential impact on these. Some research has found that group training involving singing and the use of percussive instruments improves decoding (Douglas & Willatts, 1994; Moreno et al., 2009) while other research has shown improvements in phonological awareness but no improvement in decoding skills (Gromko, 2005; Overy, 2003). These differences might be explained by the different types of musical training and the different ages and reading levels of the participating children. The development of phonological skills may be important early on and enhanced with shorter periods of musical engagement whereas longer training may be needed to influence decoding. However, Corrigall and Trainor (2011), examining the association between length of music training and reading ability in 46 6- 9 year old children enrolled in music lessons, found that length of training correlated significantly with reading comprehension but was not associated with word decoding scores. The length of music training was robustly associated with reading comprehension even after age and socioeconomic status, auditory perception, word decoding, general intelligence and the number of hours spent reading each week were taken into account.

One strand of research has focused on children who are experiencing difficulties with reading. Nicholson (1972) studied the impact of a music intervention on students aged between 6- 8 categorised as slow learners. After music training the experimental group exhibited significantly higher reading scores scoring in the eighty eighth percentile versus the seventy second percentile. After an additional year of musical training the reading scores of the experimental group were still superior to those of the control group. Movsesian (1967) found similar results with students in first, second and third grade. Thomson (2014) investigated the perception of amplitude envelopes in speech/non speech and the necessity of this skill for parsing the sounds represented as letters in literacy in a group of school children with dyslexia. A six week rhythm based intervention had positive effects on phonological awareness and literacy equal to those of a control intervention on phonemic awareness. Long (2014) studied fifteen children identified as poor readers by their school. They received ten minutes of rhythmic training weekly which included stamping, clapping and chanting to a beat and simple notation. The children demonstrated statistically significant gains in reading comprehension, accuracy and rate of reading. Comprehension and rate of reading had large effect sizes with a moderate effect size for accuracy. Miendlarewska and Trost (2014) in a review suggest that rhythmic entrainment is an essential mechanism supporting the learning and development of executive functions which may underlie enhancements in reading and verbal memory.

Overall, the direct evidence in relation to musical activities contributing to the enhancement of reading skills is mixed. There do seem to be benefits for engaging in musical activities in relation to reading beyond those associated with language development but our understanding of these processes is currently limited. Expert reading is a complex skill which depends on decoding as a prerequisite for comprehension. Decoding requires phonological skills. There is considerable evidence as outlined above that music supports the development of these skills. If children are unable to decode the extent to which they can understand text will be very limited. If aural language skills are already well developed, any musical activity may need to focus on reading musical notation for transfer benefits to occur in relation to reading where there are parallels with reading text from left to right and the matching of symbols with sounds.

The different outcomes of the research may also be partly explained by the different methods used to assess reading and the nature of the musical interventions and experiences of the participants, for instance, whether they support the development of pitch, melodic or rhythmic skills. Pitch perception has been found to be associated with reading ability in five year olds after controlling for non-verbal ability (Lamb & Gregory, 1993) and in seven to ten year old reading disabled children after controlling for general intelligence (Barwick et al., 1989), while Besson and colleagues (2007) examined pitch processing in dyslexic children and found that they had difficulties discriminating strong pitch changes that were easily discriminated by normal readers.

There is some evidence that rhythmic skills may be a better predictor of reading ability than pitch based skill (Douglas & Willatts, 1994; Huss et al., 2011; Strait, et al., 2011a; 2011b), although not all of the research supports this. There is a relationship between tests of auditory-visual rhythmic pattern matching and reading ability in eight and nine year olds (Rudnick et al., 1967; Sterrit & Rudnick, 1967). Douglas and Willatts (1994) found that rhythm processing but not pitch processing correlated with reading and spelling abilities after accounting for vocabulary scores in normal achieving readers. Lipscomb and colleagues (2008) provided a form of reading rhythmic training to children in third grade who participated in four sessions each week for 12 weeks where they read lists of words at varying tempi. This led to a dramatic improvement in reading fluency. Moritz and colleagues (2013) studying kindergarten children explored the relationship between rhythmic skills, phonological awareness and segmentation of phonemes. Rhythm perception was related to phonological awareness and basic word identification skills. Moritz and colleagues argued that rhythm sensitivity is a pre-curser to oral language acquisition and the ability to perceive and manipulate time intervals in sound streams and that this may link the performance of rhythm and phonological tasks. Schon (2014) has also shown that phonological awareness can be influenced by several months of rhythmic training which in turn improves reading skills.

The evidence for the importance of rhythmic training is especially strong for poor or dyslexic readers (Overy, 2000; 2003; Tallal et al., 1993; Thomson, 1993). Huss and colleagues (2011) have shown that dyslexics have lower performance than normal achieving readers on tasks involving musical metrical structure. This is supported by a range of studies showing that they have difficulties with keeping a beat (Corriveau et al., 2007; Corriveau & Goswami, 2009; Goswami et al., 2002; Tierney & Kraus, 2013; Wolff et al., 1990). While they have impaired rhythmic processing skills, especially for rhythm production, they have normal pitch processing skills (Overy, 2000; 2003; Overy et al., 2003). Long (2014) showed that significant gains occurred in poor readers' comprehension, reading accuracy and reading rate following rhythmic training. An analysis of reading fluency revealed significant gains in the prosodic features of reading behaviour, highlighting syllable division, grammatical structures and phrase contours. She argued that the outcomes could have been the result of changes in several processes. The rhythmic training may have facilitated the natural tendency in English to apply a stress-timed pattern, have generated a self-sustaining momentum, may have helped the children to track the direction, length and shape of the phrases embedded within the melodic and harmonic structure of the musical accompaniment or may have had an activatory effect for the sharpened definition of phonemes in terms of prosodic attributes in their relative positions in adjacent syllables on sub-cortical automatic language processing mechanisms.

Some studies have reported the importance of both rhythmic and pitch perception in the development of reading skills (Atterbury, 1985; Forgeard et al., 2008). Atterbury (1985) found that reading-disabled children aged 7-9 could discriminate rhythm patterns as well as controls but were poorer in rhythm performance and tonal memory than normal-achieving readers. Anvari and colleagues (2002) studied 50 four and 50 five year olds and found that both rhythm and pitch perception skills predicted early reading performance in four year olds even after taking account of variance due to phonological awareness. In five year olds only pitch perception predicted early reading performance after accounting for phonological awareness. Tsang and Conrad (2011) studied 69 children with and without formal music training. The trained children outperformed the untrained children on pitch discrimination, rhythm discrimination and phonological skills, although the two groups performed the same on tests of word identification, timbre discrimination and receptive vocabulary.

Where musical activities involve learning to read notation there may be direct transfer to reading text. Singing as it involves reading predicable text, segmenting words into syllables so that lyrics can be matched to music or recognising patterns has been proposed as one possible explanation for the improvement of literacy following musical activity (e.g. Butzlaff, 2000; Forgeard et al., 2008).

Other possible explanations for the impact of musical training on reading performance relate to changes in concentration and motivation. For instance, it has been proposed that music training teaches children motivational and concentration skills that help them focus for long periods of time helping them to persevere (Butzlaff, 2000). Strait and colleagues (2011a; 2011b) assessed auditory working memory and attention, music aptitude, reading ability and neural sensitivity to acoustic regularities in 42 school aged children with a wide range of reading skills. Structural equation modelling showed that music aptitude and literacy both related to the extent of sub-cortical adaptation to regularities in ongoing speech as well as with auditory working memory and attention. The findings emphasised the importance of rhythmic regularity for both language and music.

In summary, while the precise nature of the relationships between musical training and reading skills are currently unclear there is sufficient accruing evidence to suggest that musical training which supports the development of pitch and rhythmic skills supports the development of fluent reading leading to enhanced comprehension.

Spelling

There has been much less focus on the impact of active engagement with music on spelling compared with reading. In an early study, Douglas and Willatts (1994), working with seven and eight year olds, found positive correlations among tests of pitch and rhythmic aptitude, vocabulary, reading and spelling. When vocabulary scores were taken into account the association between rhythm and spelling abilities remained but those between pitch aptitude and spelling disappeared suggesting the importance of rhythm in relation to spelling. Overy (2003) found a positive effect of music lessons on spelling performance with children with poor spelling skills benefitting the most, while Hille and colleagues (2011) tested 194 boys who were in Grade 3 (aged 8-9 years) in Germany just over half of whom had learned to play a musical instrument. The boys who played an instrument showed better performance in spelling an effect which occurred independently of intelligence test scores, there being only a weak correlation between spelling mistakes and non-verbal measures of intelligence. Examination of data from those who performed poorly on spelling showed that those who played an instrument were under-represented. Only twenty-seven per cent of boys in the lowest quartile played an instrument whereas sixty-one per cent of boys in the highest quartiles were active musicians. Singing in a choir or taking part in a course entitled 'First Experiences with music' were not associated with spelling performance suggesting that it was skills developed through playing an instrument which had the potential for transfer. Currently, there is insufficient research on the relationship between actively engaging in musical activities and spelling skills to draw any firm conclusions.

Writing

As with spelling, little attention has been paid to the the influence of active engagement with music on writing. An exception was a study where children from economically disadvantaged homes participated in instruction which focused on the concepts of print, singing activities and writing. The children in the experimental group showed enhanced print concepts and pre-writing skills (Standley & Hughes, 1997). Register (2001, 2004) replicated this work with a larger sample of children. The results again showed a marked positive effect for those participating in the music-enhanced instruction in writing skills and print awareness. In contrast, a more recent study (Rickard et al., 2012) found a negative effect on writing for those participating in musical activities when compared with controls. As yet the jury is out as to whether there is any relationship between developing musical skills and writing skills.

Aural and visual memory

Musical training has been found to enhance auditory memory for a range of musical sounds and patterns (Aleman et al., 2000; Fujioka et al., 2004) and for related material including remembering spoken and sung song lyrics (Kilgour et al., 2000). In addition to this, verbal memory advantages have been found in professional musicians in relation to remembering prose passages (Jakobson et al., 2003) and a range of other verbal stimuli, for instance, memory for strings of digits or lists of words or non-words (Hanna-Pladdy & Gajewski, 2012; Hansen et al., 2013; Roden et al., 2014a) and short excerpts of speech (Cohen et al., 2011). When required to recall items in an order different from that in which they are presented, for example backwards, musicians also outperform non musicians when words or numbers are presented aurally (Parbery-Clark et al., 2011; Strait et al., 2012). Overall, there is a growing body of evidence that musical training stimulates aural memory.

In early studies, Chan and colleagues (Chan et al., 1998; Chan & Cheung, 1998) showed that learning to play a musical instrument enhanced the ability to remember words. Participants with musical training could remember seventeen per cent more verbal information than those without musical training. Ho and colleagues (2003) supported these findings in a later study of 90 6-15 year old boys. Those with musical training had significantly better verbal learning and retention abilities. Duration of music training (learning to play an instrument) and verbal learning performance correlated positively even after controlling for age and education level. Those with musical training learned approximately twenty per cent more words from a 16 word list. Their retention was also better after 10 and 30 minute delays. A follow up study, compared children from the same cohort who had just begun or continued their music training for one year and those who had given up. Children in the beginner and advanced training groups significantly increased verbal learning and retention performance. This was not the case for those who had discontinued training, although their verbal memory performance remained stable at least nine months after ceasing to play an instrument. Ho and colleagues concluded that music training seemed to have long-term enhancing effects on verbal memory. Since this early work a number of studies have found similar relationships between auditory working memory and musical training (e.g. Bidelman et al., 2013; Brandler & Rammsayer, 2003; George & Coch, 2011; Jakobson et al., 2008; Lee et al., 2007; Oechslin et al., 2013; Parbery-Clark et al., 2009a; 2009b; 2011; Rickard et al., 2010; Roden et al., 2012; Strait & Kraus, 2011a; 2011b; Strait et al., 2010; Stupar, 2012).

In a typical intervention study, Rickard and colleagues (2010) investigated 142 children from nine primary schools, 82 of whom had participated in an enhanced school-based music programme. The remainder of the children acted as controls and received standard class music education. The children were tested three times within the first two years of the study and in the third year a subset of the control sample were tested again. Verbal learning and immediate recall scores significantly increased after one year of enhanced school-based music training. No such increase was found in the control group. However, these advantages disappeared in the second year, although in the second year of the study there was significantly enhanced visual perception for the music training group.

In a similar study, Roden and colleagues (2014a) investigated the influence of group instrumental training on the working memory of children learning instruments through a German Sistema inspired programme. A quasi experimental design was used with children receiving musical training compared with those receiving natural science training or no training. The music group received weekly lessons for 45 minutes on musical instruments of their choice. The maximum group size was five and the children could undertake practice at home. The children were tested at three points over the course of 18 months with a battery of tests including seven subtests which addressed the central executive, the phonological loop and the visuospatial sketchpad components of Baddeley's working memory model. The music group showed a greater increase on every measure of verbal memory (verbal learning, delayed recall, recognition) than the science and control groups. There were large effect sizes. These differences remained when the statistical modelling took into account age and measured intelligence.

Overall, the evidence suggests that children who have musical training develop efficient memory strategies for verbal materials. This is likely to be because playing music requires continued monitoring of meaningful chunks of information. Individual notes are combined into meaningful melodic phrases which have a quasi-syllabic structure and are based on temporal frameworks that have metric structures which parallel stresses on syllables in language (Patel & Daniele 2003). This analysis is supported by evidence that the auditory cortex is structurally and functionally shaped through the individual's experiences with sound (Fritz et al., 2007). It seems that musicians' enhanced perceptual skills and the relationships between auditory working memory, attention and auditory brainstem properties are developed in a top-down manner through training (Strait et al., 2012).

In relation to the impact of musical training on visual memory, early work focused on memory for musical notation. Sloboda (1976) showed that musically trained adults showed significantly greater capacity to maintain musical notation in short-term memory than non-musicians. However, when the impact of musical training on visual memory more generally is considered the evidence is mixed. Some studies have indicated that musical training can enhance visual memory for material which is not musical text (e.g. Brochard et al., 2004; Costa-Giomi, 1999; Gardiner et al., 1996; George & Coch, 2011; Hanna-Pladdy & MacKay, 2011; Hetland, 2000; Jakobson et al., 2003; 2008; Lee et al., 2007; Rauscher et al., 1995; Sluming et al., 2007; Stoesz et al., 2007), while other studies do not support this (e.g. Brandler and Rammsayer, 2003; Chan et al., 1998; Hanna-Pladdy & Gajewski, 2012; Ho et al., 2003; Rickard et al., 2010; Roden et al., 2012; 2014a).

There are a number of reasons why the evidence relating to visual memory may be inconsistent. Firstly, the research has assessed visual memory using different methods including reaction times and recall accuracy. Participants in early studies (Chan et al., 1998; Ho et al., 2003) were Chinese where the nature of the written language meant that the experimental and control groups were already skilled in processing complex visual signs so that the musical training may have had less impact. Participants in the research have also varied between children and adults. The nature of the musical training itself may also be important, particularly the extent to which it involves learning to read musical notation. For instance, Degé and colleagues (2011b) tested the effect of an extended music curriculum for two years in secondary school on children's visual and auditory memory. The curriculum consisted of learning to play a musical instrument including participating in an orchestra, auditory perception and music theory training. Ten year old children who had just started the programme and children without training were tested on visual and aural memory at the start of the programme and two years later. Prior to the training there were no differences between the groups but the children engaged with the musical training improved significantly from time one to time two in visual and auditory memory while the children not receiving training did not. These effects were apparent even when a range of confounding variables was taken into account in the analysis including intelligence, socio-economic status, extra-curricular schooling, motivation to avoid work, and musical aptitude. To summarise it seems that musical training has a consistent positive impact on aural memory and in some circumstances, which may depend on the type of musical activity engaged with, may have an impact on visual memory.

Susan Hallam

Spatial reasoning and mathematical performance

Spatial reasoning

There is considerable evidence from research with professional musicians that they have better spatial abilities than non-musicians including mental rotation (Pietsch & Jansen, 2012; Sluming et al., 2007), visuo-spatial search tasks (Patston & Tippett, 2011; Rodrigues et al., 2013; Stoesz et al., 2007) and reaction times to selective and divided visual attention tasks (Rodrigues et al., 2013). They are also better at matching a set of coloured blocks to a visual image (Stoesz et al., 2007), have better memory for line drawings (Jakobson et al., 2008) and are more accurate when asked to mark the centre of a horizontal line (Patston et al., 2006) and to judge the orientation of a line (Patston et al., 2007). However, these correlation studies do not necessarily indicate that musical engagement has enhanced these skills. It may be that musicians already have strong spatial skills which contribute to the development of their musical skills.

Some research has examined the impact of specific music interventions on spatial reasoning in children in an attempt to establish causality. There is evidence that general music instruction, including singing, movement, and playing percussion instruments can assist children in the development of spatial ability (Bilhartz et al., 1999; Persellin, 2000) as can having piano lessons over a period of a year (Zafranas, 2004). In a review of 15 studies Hetland (2000) found a 'strong and reliable' relationship and concluded that music instruction leads to dramatic improvements in performance on spatial-temporal measures. She commented on the consistency of the effects and likened them to differences of one inch in height or about 84 points on the SAT (p 221). She showed that the effects were likely to be stronger among younger children (3-5 years) than those aged 6-12 years. The consistency of these findings suggests a near transfer, automated effect.

Other studies offer further support. Rauscher and colleagues (1997) assigned 78 students from three preschools to music, computer or no instruction groups. The instruction groups received training in either piano keyboard (individually) coupled with group singing lessons, group singing lessons only or computer instruction. The children were pre and post tested using one spatial temporal reasoning task (object assembly) and three spatial recognition tasks (geometric design, block design and animal pegs). There were no differences between groups in pretest scores but after instruction the children in the piano group scored significantly higher on the spatial reasoning task compared to children in the other conditions. There were no differences amongst the groups on the spatial recognition tasks. The computer, group singing and no instruction groups did not improve significantly over time on any of the tests. Later studies (Rauscher, 2002; Rauscher & Zupan, 2000) undertaken over three years with upper-middle income children who were provided with eight months of weekly 40 minute keyboard instruction in groups of 8 - 10 beginning in either kindergarten (aged 5) or first grade (aged 6) scored higher on two spatial temporal tasks, puzzle solving and block building compared to children who did not receive music instruction. No enhancement was found for a pictorial memory task. However, the effects were not maintained when music instruction was terminated, although when lessons resumed in second grade the same children's scores increased again surpassing the levels that they had reached before the lessons were terminated. The children who received instruction over a period of three years scored higher on the spatial temporal tasks compared to children who had not received instruction. While the scores of the keyboard group improved every year although not significantly, after kindergarten the scores of children who began instruction in the second grade did not improve suggesting that it was important that the training began early. Further studies examined the effects of musical instruction on spatial temporal reasoning in middle income elementary school children (see Rauscher & Hinton, 2011). Two groups, a music group and an animated reading group received 40 minutes of lessons in groups of 8-10 for nine months. At the end of the study children who received the keyboard lessons scored significantly higher than those who received the animated reading lessons but the improvement for the keyboard group was only for girls.

Another strand of research has focused on pre-school children from deprived backgrounds participating in Head Start programmes (Rauscher, 2003, Rauscher et al., 2005). In the first study, 87 Head Start children were assigned randomly to one of three groups, piano, computer or no instruction for 48 weeks over two years. At the end of the intervention the children who received music instruction scored significantly higher than the control groups on visual and auditory tasks that required spatial and temporal skills. Performance on an arithmetic task also improved following music instruction. A second study focused on whether different types of music instruction had different effects. Over 100 Head Start children of mixed ethnicity were assigned randomly to one of four conditions, piano, singing, rhythm or no instruction. All the children in the music groups received weekly individual instruction for a period of 48 weeks over two years. The data from the three music groups replicated the data from the first study. The children in the music groups scored significantly higher at post test on tasks requiring spatial and temporal skills. The rhythm group scored significantly higher than the piano and singing groups on the temporal and arithmetic tasks. A third study was conducted to determine whether the effects endured after instruction stopped. The scores of the Head Start children who received lessons in the first and second studies were compared with three groups of grade matched children participating in Head Start who did not receive music instruction, at-risk children not involved in Head Start, and middle income children who did not receive music instruction. The children who had received music instruction in the first study continued to score higher than all other groups of children, with the exception of the age matched middle income children, on three of the four tests two years after instruction had ended. The data from the children who participated in the second study when they progressed to kindergarten showed that the singing, piano and rhythm groups scored higher than the Head Start and at-risk children on five of the tests. In addition, the rhythm group scored higher than the singing and piano groups on an arithmetic subtest and scored significantly higher than the middle income children on the temporal, arithmetic, mathematical reasoning and numeracy tasks. These findings suggested that rhythm instruction has the strongest impact on a range of mathematically related tasks. Further evidence for music being responsible for enhanced spatial reasoning in at-risk children comes from an Israeli study in which a two year music training intervention (2-3 hours per week) was introduced in some after-school centres for at-risk children but not in other centres (Portowitz et al., 2007). Children participating in the intervention showed larger improvements in remembering and re-producing a complex line drawing.

The quality of the musical input is crucial in any transfer of skills. This was illustrated in a three year study to explore whether group music instruction could improve the test scores of economically disadvantaged elementary school children which included almost 600 kindergarten through fifth grade students from four elementary schools. One school provided 30 minutes of keyboard lessons per week, another a 40 minute lesson every six days, while the remaining two schools acted as controls. All lessons were in groups of 20-25 pupils. Pupils were pre-tested with two subtests measuring verbal abilities, two measuring quantitative abilities and one measuring spatial temporal abilities. Tests were then repeated at 9, 18 and 27 months. During the first two years of the study there were difficulties in the implementation of the music programme and it was only at the end of the study when the children had received one year of high quality tuition that there were any gains for the students (Rauscher, 2005).

Taken together, the evidence suggests that active engagement in musical activities enhances a range of spatial processing skills. Why this is the case and which particular musical activities are implicated requires further investigation.

Mathematical performance

Historically, there has long been interest in the relationship between acquired musical skills and performance in mathematics as it has been assumed that there is a strong connection between music and mathematics as musicians play from notation and are constantly required to adopt quasi-mathematical processes to sub-divide beats and turn rhythmic notation into sound. However, the evidence is mixed and some of it is negative.

In an early example, Pannenborg and Pannenborg (1915) compared individuals with varying degrees of musical talent and found only a slightly higher level of mathematical ability in those with high levels of musical ability. In a survey of 227 musical and 72 unmusical male participants, Haecker and Ziehen (1922) found that only two percent reported being mathematically talented. Revesz (1954) also found reported levels of interest or aptitude for mathematics in musicians was low with inconclusive findings.

Vaughn (2000) meta-analyzed studies comparing mathematics achievement in students with and without self-selected music study and only reported a very small positive association (r = .13). In a relatively recent study, Haimson and colleagues (2011a; 2011b) recruited participants from the online membership of the American Mathematical Society and the Modern Language Association and presented them with a questionnaire assessing skills in musicality and musicianship. Members of both groups reported relatively low levels of musicality with no statistically significant differences between them. In contrast, a study using a national data base in the United States of America found positive effects on mathematical performance for engagement with music. Catterall and colleagues (1999) using the NELS:88 data compared low socioeconomic status students who exhibited high math proficiency in the twelfth grade and found that thirty three percent were involved in instrumental music compared with fifteen percent who were not involved. Focusing on children learning to play an instrument, Haley (2001) also found that those who had studied an instrument prior to fourth grade had higher scores in mathematics than those in other groups.

Some studies have explored the impact of specific musical training on mathematics skills. Graziano and colleagues (1999) reported that piano keyboard training along with computer based spatial training led to greater improvements in mathematics than when the same spatial training was combined with computer based English language training. Gardiner and colleagues (1996) showed that children participating in an arts program which included music with a lower score on mathematics at baseline outperformed controls in terms of mathematics achievement, those participating the longest having the highest scores overall. Geoghegan and Mitchelmore (1996) investigated the impact of a weekly early childhood music program on the mathematics achievement of preschool children aged 4-5 years. The group of children involved in musical activities scored higher on a mathematics achievement test than the control group, although home musical background may have been a confounding factor. The children who listened more frequently to adults singing and their own music collection at home performed better than other children. Rickard and colleagues (2012) found that mathematics scores increased for children receiving additional music training when compared with controls but indicated that the effects were relatively small. Rauscher and Hinton (2011) provided a summary of results from several studies which focused on the impact of music lessons on preschoolers from low socio-economic staturs families randomly allocated to two years of music lessons and compared them to control groups assigned to computer lessons or no lessons. At the end of the study, the music groups had higher scores on arithmetic and spatial abilities although they were equivalent initially. Courey and colleagues (2012) in a study focusing on understanding of fractions assigned third grade children to a general mathematics programme or academic music instruction twice a week for 45 minutes over six weeks. Those in the music group used their conceptual understanding of music to inform their solutions to fraction computational problems. There were statistically significant differences in the performance of the two groups with large effect sizes. Those students who initially had less knowledge about fractions responded well to the music initiative and produced post-intervention scores similar to those of existing high achievers. Johnson and Edelson (2003) also implemented an activity for teaching children aspects of mathematics through musical concepts using musical instruments and musical symbols to expand concepts of serial order, fractions, sorting, classification and ratios. They concluded that music had the potential to assist in developing mathematical skills. However, in a study examining whether children's experience of music training related to mathematics and their performance on a musical achievement test Yang and colleagues (2014) found that while there was a relationship this did not appear to be causal. Similarly, Rafferty (2003) found no effect of the Music Spatial-Temporal Maths Program on the mathematics achievement of second graders and Costa-Giomi (2004) showed a negative effect on mathematical computation. A recent systematic review supports the inconclusive nature of the findings (Jaschke et al., 2013).

One of the reasons for the low levels of association between musical training and mathematics may be that musical training is associated with some aspects of mathematics but not others. For instance, Bahna-James (1991) found that high-school students' music theory grades correlated with their grades in algebra, geometry and pre-calculus but not with grades on an advanced mathematics course on logic. Similarly, Bahr and Christensen (2000) reported that performance on a mathematics test and a musicianship rating scale correlated in areas where music and maths shared structural overlap in pattern recognition and symbol usage but not for other areas of mathematics where there was no overlap. However, not all of the research supports this. For instance, Helmbold and colleagues (2005) failed to demonstrate any advantage for musicians in pattern recognition.

The type of musical training may be important. Cheek and Smith (1999) studying eighth graders found that those who had two or more years of private lessons had higher mathematics scores, while those learning keyboard instruments had higher scores than those learning other instruments. Another factor may be length of engagement. Whitehead (2001) found that middle and high school students who were placed in high, moderate and no treatment groups for music instruction differed in mathematics gains, the high involvement children showing the greatest gains.

Overall, the evidence suggests that active engagement with music may be able to improve some elements of mathematical performance, but the nature of this relationship, the kinds of musical training needed to realise the effect, the length of time required and the specific types of mathematical problems which are affected need further investigation.

Intellectual development

There has long been an interest in the relationship between musical training and intellectual development. Many early studies explored the relationships between the two with a particular focus on how intelligence mediated musical ability (Beckham, 1942; Fracker and Howard, 1928; Hollingworth, 1926). Later studies explored the relationships (e.g. Antrim, 1945; Bienstock, 1942; Ross, 1936) not addressing the direction of causality which has led some to argue that more intelligent children are drawn to participate in musical activities (Farnsworth, 1946; Ross, 1936). Indeed there is evidence that children who take up a musical instrument frequently have higher level academic skills prior to participating in musical activities (Feldman & Matjasko, 2005; Fitzpatrick, 2006; Gibson et al., 2009; Hille et al., 2011; Kinney, 2008, 2010; 2007; Ruthsatz et al., 2008; Schellenberg, 2011a; Schellenberg & Mankarious, 2012), although this is not always the case (Habibi et al., 2014). Take up is often related to the socio-economic status of families and family make-up both of which support opportunities for musical engagement (Bugaj & Brenner, 2011; Costa-Giomi, 2012; Elpus & Abril, 2011; Kinney, 2010; Schellenberg & Weiss, 2013).

Research which has adopted a retrospective approach to studying the relationship between active engagement with music and intelligence has found enhanced performance from musicians on a range of intellectual skills. For instance, adopting a cross sectional approach, Schlaug and colleagues (2005) compared 9-11 year old instrumentalists with an average of four years training with controls. They showed that the instrumental group performed significantly better than the control group on musical audiation, left hand index finger tapping rate, and the vocabulary subtest of the WISC-III. Strong non-significant trends were seen in a phonemic awareness test, Raven's Progressive Matrices, and a mathematics test.

Schellenberg and colleagues have undertaken a series of studies exploring the relationships between musical engagement and intelligence. For instance, Schellenberg (2006) administered standardized tests of intelligence to a sample of about 300 children and adults. Participants varied widely in the extent of their musical experiences outside school. Among the children cognitive performance was associated positively with months of music lessons even after holding constant parents' education, family income, and duration of involvement. Associations were strongest for an aggregate measure of intelligence with no association between musical activity and particular subtests when general intelligence was held constant.

In a later study, Schellenberg (2011a) compared 106 children aged 9-12 in terms of their musical training and IQ scores (Wechsler Abbreviated Scale of Intelligence including vocabulary, block design, similarities and matrix reasoning). The musically trained children had higher IQ scores which remained when a range of socio-economic factors were taken into account. However, in a study of pitch processing and general intelligence, Schellenberg and Moreno (2010) found that trained participants exhibited superior performance on tests of pitch-processing speed and relative pitch but no superiority on a measure of general intelligence.

Hille and colleagues (2011) explored the impact of different types of musical activities on intelligence. They tested 194 boys aged 8-9 years just over half of whom had learned to play a musical instrument. Non-verbal measures of intelligence were higher for boys playing an instrument with a moderate effect size, but no difference in non-verbal measures of intelligence was found for boys who sang in a choir and those who did not. Overall, active participation in a choir or lessons called 'First Experiences with Music' did not show the benefits associated with learning to play an instrument.

Intervention studies have demonstrated the complexity of the issues involved. In an early study Hurwitz and colleagues (1975) assigned first-grade children to a group receiving Kodaly music lessons for five days each week for seven months or a control group which did not. At the end of the study, the experimental group scored significantly higher than the control group on three of five sequencing tasks and four of five spatial tasks. No statistically significant differences were found for verbal measures, although the children in the experimental group had higher reading achievement scores than those in the control group which were maintained after two academic years. Gromko and Poorman (1998) compared pre-school children in a group engaging in weekly musical activities with a control group and found that for the three year olds in the study an intellectually stimulating environment resulted in a gain in the ability to perform the spatial-temporal task element of an intelligence test. Bilhartz and colleagues (1999) studied the relationship between participation in a structured music curriculum and cognitive development in 4-6 year olds. Half of the children participated in a 30 week 75 minute weekly parent-involved music curriculum. Following this, children were tested with six sub-tests of the Stanford-Binet intelligence test and the Young Child Music Skills Assessment test. There were significant gains for the music group on the music test and the Stanford-Binet Bead Memory subtest.

Costa-Giomi (1999, 2004, Costa-Giomi and Ryan, 2007) completed a longitudinal study on the effects of piano instruction on children's cognitive abilities. Children were randomly assigned to an experimental or a control group. Each child received free instruction. The two groups of children were comparable at the start of the study in terms of musical ability, cognitive abilities, and academic achievement in maths and language and motor skills. After two years of instruction the children in the experimental group obtained significantly higher scores on the cognitive ability tests and the spatial scores but no differences were found after three years. No differences in the quantitative and verbal cognitive abilities of the two groups were found after two years of the study. A follow up study conducted seven years after the completion of the lessons showed no differences between groups. Similarly, analysis at the ten year follow up (Costa-Giomi and Ryan, 2007) showed no differences in IQ or memory. The initial gains became negligible over time. The improvements were small and temporary and seem to have depended on the level of the children's commitment and effort. After three years, twenty two percent of the variance in cognitive improvement was explained by their attendance at lessons and time spent practising. Those who were more committed gained more (Costa-Giomi, 1999).

In a carefully controlled study, Schellenberg (2004) randomly assigned a large sample of children to four different groups, two of which received music lessons (standard keyboard, Kodaly voice) for a year, the control groups receiving instruction in a non-musical artistic activity (drama) or no lessons. All four groups exhibited increases in IQ as would be expected over the time period but the music groups had reliably larger increases in full scale IQ with an effect size of .35. Children in the control groups had average increases of 4.3 points while the music groups had increases of seven points. On all but two of the 12 subtests the music group had larger increases than control groups. Notably, the music groups had larger increases on the four indexes that measured more specific abilities (verbal ability, spatial ability, processing speed, and attention).

Another study focused on Iranian kindergarteners who were assigned randomly to twelve 75 minute music lessons taught weekly and compared to children of the same age matched on gender and socioeconomic status who did not receive lessons (Kaviani et al., 2014). The music group had larger increases in IQ over the 12-week period. Similarly, a study with Israeli children aged 6-12 found a causal effect of music training on intelligence. Children who were assigned to a two-year music-training program had larger increases in general intelligence compared to a control group with no intervention (Portowitz & Klein, 2007; Portowitz et al., 2009).

In a more recent study, Moreno and colleagues (2011a; 2011b) devised two interactive computerised training programmes with a focus on music or art. After only 20 days of training the children in the music group exhibited enhanced performance on a measure of verbal intelligence. These changes were positively correlated with changes in functional brain plasticity during an executive function task which the authors suggested indicated that the impact of musical engagement on intelligence was related to executive functions.

Not all of the intervention research has supported the findings showing increases in IQ relating to active participation in musical activities. Mehr and colleagues (2013) conducted two random controlled trials with American preschool children aged four years comparing participation in music classes with visual arts classes. Parents attended classes with their children. The classes ran for six weeks with a total of 4.5 hours of musical engagement. The musical engagement involved singing, some work with percussion instruments and movement and was relatively unstructured. The children were tested in four distinctive cognitive areas, spatial-navigational reasoning, visual form analysis, numerical discrimination, and receptive vocabulary. In the first experiment the children from the music group showed greater spatial navigational ability while children from the visual arts class showed greater visual form analysis. However, a partial replication with another group of children did not confirm these findings.

A key issue arising from this research is the nature of the musical activity which brings about change in relation to particular aspects of intellectual development and why. The research reported above was based on children's participation in a variety of musical activities, some offering a broad musical education, others focused more closely on instrumental tuition. To begin to address these questions, Rauscher and colleagues (reported in Rauscher, 2009) explored the impact of different types of musical activity in at-risk preschool children. Five groups received piano, singing, rhythm, computer or no instruction for two years. The three music groups scored higher following instruction than the control groups on mental imagery tasks but the scores of the rhythm group were significantly higher than all other groups on tasks requiring temporal cognition and mathematical ability. The findings from this study suggest that it is rhythmic training which is important for the development of temporal cognition and mathematics skills, while developing enhanced perceptual skills in relation to pitch and melody supports language development, although rhythm emerges as important in relation to literacy.

Despite the conflicting evidence from intervention studies, it seems that engagement with music can enhance some skills which contribute to scores on intelligence tests. The evidence suggests that the longer the training the greater the impact (Corrigall & Schellenberg, 2014; Corrigall et al., 2013; Degé et al., 2011a; Degé et al., 2014; Schellenberg, 2006) and that the relationships between musical training and intelligence remain when a range of confounding variables related to family background are taken into account in the analyses (Corrigall et al., 2013; Degé et al., 2011a; Schellenberg, 2006, 2011a, 2011b, Schellenberg & Mankarious, 2012). Catterall and Rauscher (2008) argue that the gains seen in more general IQ are likely to be the result of specific gains in visual-spatial intelligence but there may also be effects related to the enhanced development of language and literacy skills. Črnčec and colleagues in a review (2006) concluded that music instruction conferred consistent benefits for spatio-temporal reasoning skills; however, improvements in associated academic domains, such as arithmetic, had not been reliably shown. Jaschke and colleagues (2013) in review of research on children aged 4-13 argued that there was a need to clarify the nature of the research questions being considered and whether global or subsets of measures of intelligence should be used.

Overall, taking the findings together, it would appear that active engagement with making music can have an impact on intellectual development. What requires further research is the specific types of musical participation which develop specific skills which may transfer automatically to other areas and what are the common features of these skills.

Executive functioning and self-regulation

One explanation for the impact of musical activities on intellectual skills draws on the possible mediating role of executive functioning and self-regulation. Executive functions are related to working memory and also involve the conscious control of action, thoughts, emotions and general abilities such as planning, the capacity to ignore irrelevant information, to inhibit incorrect automatic responses and to solve problems. Executive functions also include cognitive flexibility - the ability to adjust to novel or changing task demands (Diamond, 1990; 2002; Lezak, 2004; Zelazo, 2004). Executive functions are predominantly located in the frontal cortex. A recent model of intelligence, parieto-frontal integration theory (P-FIT) (Jung & Haier, 2007) has highlighted structural links common to music, language and intelligence specifically in shared brain structures such as the prefrontal cortex, the anterior cingulated and a region within the temporal lobes.

Playing a musical instrument, particularly in an ensemble requires many sub-skills associated with executive functioning including sustained attention, goal-directed behaviour and cognitive flexibility. Formal music practice involves cognitive challenge, controlled attention for long periods of time, keeping musical passages in working memory or encoding them into long-term memory and decoding musical scores and translating them into motor programmes. These activities draw on complex cognitive functions which have been illustrated in brain imaging research (Schon et al., 2002; Stewart et al., 2003). Hannon and Trainor (2007) argue that formal musical instruction seems to train a set of attentional and executive functions, which have domain-specific and domain-general consequences. The development process for this to occur is complex as plasticity is affected by various anatomical processes, such as synaptic proliferation and pruning, myelination, and neurofilament and neurotransmitter levels, each of which has its own developmental trajectory. As learning proceeds neural networks settle into more stable states. What is clear is that executive functions are imperative for learning and impact on academic attainment at all levels (Best et al., 2011).

Correlation studies have explored the relationships between active music making and enhanced executive functioning. Studies of adult musicians have shown superiority in terms of some executive functions when compared with non-musicians, for instance in non-verbal spatial tasks and auditory and visual Stroop tasks (Bialystok & DePape, 2009; Travis et al., 2011). Rodrigues and colleagues (2013) compared musicians working in symphony orchestras with non-musicians and found that the former had augmented ability in a range of forms of visual attention. Superior performance has been demonstrated in children and adults with musical training over non-musician controls on measures of auditory and visual working memory (e.g. Franklin et al., 2008; Fujioka et al., 2006; George & Coch, 2011; Lee et al., 2007; Pallensen et al., 2010; Parbery-Clark et al., 2011), although Meinz and Hambrick (2010) found that musical practice only accounted for about half of the variance in piano sight-reading skills with an incremental effect of working memory capacity. Processing speed has also been shown to have a positive relationship with music training in both adults (Bugos et al., 2007; Helmbold et al., 2005) and children (Roden et al., 2014b; Schellenberg, 2006). Further support for the role of executive functions comes from research showing that adult musicians are better than nonmusicians at identifying the pitch of a tone presented with conflicting but irrelevant verbal information and the direction of an arrow presented with conflicting but irrelevant spatial information (Bialystok & DePape, 2009). Working with children aged 9-12 years, with different lengths of time having music lessons, Degé and colleagues (2011a) assessed five different executive functions (set shifting, selective attention, planning, inhibition, and fluency). Significant associations emerged between music lessons and all of the measures of executive function. Executive function mediated the association between music lessons and intelligence with the measures of selective attention and inhibition being the strongest contributors to the mediation effect. The authors argued that at least part of the association between music lessons and intelligence is explained by the positive influence music lessons have on executive functions.

Not all of the research has found positive relationships between musical training, executive functions and self-regulation. Schellenberg (2011a) compared musically trained and untrained musicians aged 9-12 on a measure of IQ and five measures of executive function. IQ was measured with the Wechsler Abbreviated Scale of Intelligence (vocabulary, block design, similarities and matrix reasoning). Attention and working memory were assessed by a digit span task comprising forward and backward tasks. The test for phonological fluency asked children to name as many words as they could in one minute that started with the letter F or S. The Sun-Moon Stroop test assessed children's ability to ignore conflicting information. In the congruent task children were given pictures of suns and moons and asked to name as many as they could in 45 seconds. In the incongruent task they had to report sun for every moon and vice versa. The test of problem solving was a computerized version of the Tower of Hanoi problem. Finally, in the Wisconsin Card Sorting Test children were asked to match individual cards to a key card. They were not told how to match the cards but were given feedback after each response. The matching rule changed after 10 correct responses. The musically trained children had higher IQ scores and digit span scores which remained when a range of socioeconomic factors were taken into account but there were no differences on any of the other measures. While IQ and executive function were correlated and the musically trained group had higher IQs and this advantage extended across the IQ subtests, the association between musical training and executive function was negligible.

Evidence from neuroscience has shown that there are differences in the frontal cortex of musicians and non-musicians, the area of the brain which is implicated in the regulation of attention (Gaser & Schlaug, 2003; Sluming et al., 2002). Musical engagement increases gray matter density in the frontal brain areas which are involved in controlling musical tasks (e.g. Hyde et al., 2009), while musicians who continue to practice beyond 60 years of age show less or no degeneration of gray matter density in the frontal cortex. Practising a musical instrument seems to prevent deterioration of executive functions involving monitoring and planning (Sluming et al., 2002). Pallensen and colleagues (2010) examined working memory for musical sounds and found that in comparisons between musicians and non-musicians, the musicians had heightened activity in neuronal networks that sustained attention and cognitive control including the pre-frontal regions and the supplementary motor area. The relationship between task performance and activation patterns was strongest in the musicians during the periods when the load on working memory was the heaviest. In a recent study, Zuk and colleagues (2014) compared adults with extensive music training with non-musicians and school aged children (musicians and non-musicians) on a range of executive functions including cognitive flexibility, inhibition, verbal fluency, working memory and processing speed. The adults and the children showed heightened performance on some but not all of the executive function tests. The adults showed differences in cognitive flexibility and working memory, while the music group children showed enhanced performance on cognitive flexibility, processing speed, verbal fluency and enhanced brain activation in traditional executive function regions during rule representation and a task switching test. Nutley and colleagues (2013) focused on children and adolescents aged between six and 25 years. In a longitudinal study with testing two years apart they demonstrated that musical practice had a positive association with working memory capacity (visuo-spatial and verbal), processing speed and reasoning skills at all time points after taking into account parental education and participation in other school activities. Those participating in musical activities had larger gray matter volume in the temporo-occipital and insular cortex, areas which are known to be associated with the reading of musical notation. Changes in working memory were proportional to the number of hours spent in weekly practice but this did not apply to measures of verbal reasoning. It may be that reading notation is important in the development of at least some executive functions as it requires visuo-spatial working memory, rapid information processing, visuo-spatial decoding and a constant updating of notes.

One study has suggested that music may impact on the rate of cortical thickness maturation.

Hudziak and colleagues (2014) assessed the extent to which playing a musical instrument was associated with cortical thickness development among healthy youths. Participants (232 youths aged 6-18years) underwent MRI scanning and behavioural testing on up to three separate visits occurring at two-year intervals. While there was no association between cortical thickness and years playing a musical instrument follow-up analysis revealed that music training was associated with an increased rate of cortical thickness maturation within areas implicated in motor planning and coordination, visuospatial ability, and emotion and impulse regulation.

There is relatively little intervention research with children in relation to their executive functioning and participation in music making activities. An exception is the work of Moreno and colleagues (2011a; 2011b) who assigned 71 4-6 year-olds to four weeks of intensive computerised training in music listening or visual arts. The two programmes had the same learning goals, graphics and design, duration, number of breaks and number of teaching staff. The music curriculum was based on a combination of motor, perceptual and cognitive tasks relying primarily on listening tasks and included training in rhythm, pitch, melody, voice and basic musical concepts. The visual art curriculum focused on the development of visuo-spatial skills. The children engaged in the training programme in two daily sessions of one hour each for five days per week for four weeks. The children in the music group showed greater improvements in the ability to identify geometric figures on the basis of colour while ignoring irrelevant variation in shape. These changes were positively correlated with changes in functional brain plasticity during an executive function task. However, there was no difference in reaction times between the groups. Correlations between executive function and improvement in intelligence scores were positive and moderate. The authors argue that this suggests that any impact of musical engagement on intelligence is related to executive functions.

Other research has indicated that participation in formal early music education classes is linked with better self-regulation skills. Winsler and colleagues (2011) compared a group of 3-4 year old children receiving weekly kindermusic (music and movement) classes with a group who had not experienced any structured early childhood music classes. Those enrolled in the music classes showed better self-regulation than those not enrolled as measured by a battery of tests that required children to wait, slow down and initiate or suppress a response. The kindermusik children were also more likely to use a range of positive self-regulatory strategies including private speech during an attention task and singing/humming during a waiting task.

Parent-child music therapy efficacy studies have also indicated that joint active music participation supports improved child-parent interactions and enhanced impulse control and self-regulation skills (Malloch et al., 2012; Pasiali, 2012). Galarce and colleagues (2012) reported enhanced self-regulation in terms of inappropriate speaking to others, while Brown and Sax (2013) found that an arts enriched programme including music helped emotional regulation skills in low-income children when compared to non arts programmes.

There is a growing literature exploring the cognitive benefits of active engagement with music throughout the lifespan some of which has included self-reports which are related to executive functions. For instance, Gembris (2008) carried out a questionnaire study with members of senior amateur orchestras with an average age of 71 years and found music was seen as helping them to cope and deal with difficult situations. Participants in singing activities (Clift et al., 2008) and a wide range of musical activities (Creech et al., 2014) have also commented on the way that making music stimulates cognitive capacity including attention, concentration, memory and learning (Clift et al., 2008). Studies of older adults with high levels of musical training have shown that they tend to perform better than their musically untrained counterparts on cognitive control tasks involving nonverbal memory and cognitive flexibility (Hanna-Pladdy & MacKay, 2011) and on tasks involved in a range of auditory tasks, visuo-spatial memory span, cognitive control processes and a composite measure of cognitive control (Amer et al., 2013).

An intervention study with older adults (aged 60–85) (Bugos et al., 2007) who were randomly assigned to 6 months of individual piano lessons or a non-lessons control group found that the music group outperformed the control group on a test that assessed processing speed in matching symbols with digits. There were significant improvements in attention, concentration, planning, cognitive flexibility and working memory. For these benefits to be maintained regular practice and tuition was needed as decline followed when the activities ceased.

Overall, the jury is still out on the possible impact of music training on executive functions and their relationship with measured intelligence, although it is clear that some elements of executive functioning are enhanced by musical training. Future research needs to attempt to establish more clearly which executive functions may be implicated in transfer and whether these relate to skills which have become automated or are related to those requiring conscious cognitive processing or a combination of these.

Creativity

Researchers have paid relatively little attention to the impact of music on creativity. In early research, Simpson (1969) studying 173 high school music and 45 non-music students found that the music students scored higher on several elements of the Guildford tests of creativity. Wolff (1979) studied the effects of 30 minutes of daily music instruction for an entire year on first graders. Those participating exhibited significant increases in creativity and in perceptual motor skills compared with controls. Kalmar (1982) studied the effects of singing and musical group play twice weekly for three years on pre-school children of 3-4 years of age and found that these children scored higher than controls on creativity, had higher levels of abstraction, and showed greater creativity in improvised puppet play. They also demonstrated better motor development, while Kiehn (2003) in study of second, fourth and sixth grade children found a weak but statistically significant correlation between music creativity and figural creativity.

Major national reports on the arts have emphasised their importance in developing a range of transferable skills including those related to creativity and critical thinking (NACCCE, 1999). High school and university music students have been shown to score higher on tests of creativity than none music majors, this being particularly marked in those with more than ten years of music education (Hamann et al., 1990). Gibson and colleagues (2009) compared classical music students with other similar students on behavioural tasks also using near infrared spectroscopy. The musicians had increased convergent and divergent thinking compared with non- musicians, while the infrared spectroscopy revealed greater bilateral frontal activity in the musicians. It may be that non-musicians rely more on the left hemisphere when undertaking divergent thinking than musicians.

Comparisons of music students with those whose experiences included theatrical and visual arts showed that the music students exhibited greater creativity than controls but no effects were found for the visual arts; the greater the number of units of music classes the greater the creativity (Hamann et al., 1991). Charyton and Snelbecker (2007) investigated similarities and differences in general, artistic, and scientific creativity between higher education engineering and music students and found that the musicians scored higher in general and artistic creativity with no significant differences in scientific creativity. They also had statistically higher levels of measured general creativity, creative attributes, creative temperament, and cognitive risk tolerance.

The development of creative skills is likely to be particularly dependent on the type of musical engagement. This is supported by Koutsoupidou and Hargreaves (2009) who studied six year olds comparing those who had opportunities for musical improvisation with those where music lessons provided no opportunities for creativity. Performance on Webster's measures of Creative Thinking in Music assessed change in extensiveness, flexibility, originality, and syntax. The improvisation activities significantly supported the development of creative thinking as opposed to the didactic teaching. To enhance creativity music lessons may need to include creative activities. This is an area where further research is required.

General attainment

Most of the research exploring the links between participation in musical activities and attainment is based on correlation analysis which precludes the demonstration of causality, particularly as there are many possible confounding factors including having supportive parents and a home environment conducive to studying. There is also the possibility that music programmes may attract students who are already amongst the highest attaining (Harrison, 1990; Klinedinst, 1991), for reviews see Arnett-Gary (1998), Shobo (2001), Yoon (2000), Hodges and O'Connell (2007), Costa-Giomi (2012) and Schellenberg (2014).

The evidence from correlation studies in the USA has shown that students who participate in music education do better than their peers on many measures of academic achievement. Much of this research is based on large state wide or national datasets. For instance, at state level, Abeles (2007) reported that groups of second grade children who participated in a weekly violin programme (3 lessons every 2 weeks) outperformed non-violin group controls in performance on state wide mathematics and language arts tests. Morrison (1994) using data from the National Centre for Educational Statistics representing over 13,000 students showed that high school students who participated in music reported higher grades in English, mathematics, history, and science than those who did not participate. Similar outcomes have been reported by Trent (1996), Cardarelli (2003) and Fitzpatrick (2006). In a study of four regions of the USA, Johnson and Memmott (2006) studied 4,739 elementary and middle school students and showed a strong relationship between third and fourth grade students' academic achievement and their participation in music programmes. However, this was moderated by the quality of the programme; the higher the quality of the programme, the higher the academic attainment.

Children who have participated in music courses while in high school do better on standardized verbal and maths achievement tests in the USA with the number of years engaged in music correlated with test performance (Catterall, 1998). The most successful young musicians in the USA who participate in state wide ensembles also have higher SAT scores than state averages (DeCarbo et al., 1990; Henry & Braucht, 2007). Schellenberg (2006) showed that music training was associated positively with children's performance in school and that those who took music lessons over relatively long periods of time tended to be particularly successfully even when intelligence was controlled for.

Not all of the evidence from large scale studies supports the positive impact of participation in musical activities. Miksza (2007) using data from National Education Longitudinal Study of 1988 with a sample of 5335 created a composite item which assessed student participation in music for the entire duration of the study from eighth to twelfth grade and measured academic achievement in maths, reading comprehension, science and social studies. There were significant differences for all subtests in the initial testing in favour of those who had participated in band, choir or orchestra but rates of change in mathematics, science of social studies were no greater for the music participants and in reading achievement the music participants increased more slowly than non-participants. In a later study Miszka (2010) used data from the Educational Longitudinal Study of 2002. Multilevel modelling was able to take account of a wide range of individual factors including socio-economic status, minority status, peer influence and music participation and school level factors including the number of music teachers. Outcome variables were standardized mathematics scores, a composite community ethics score which included strong friendships, helping people in the community and working to correct social and economic inequalities and a composite school commitment variable including late arrival, skipping class and absence from school. Music participation was related to all outcome variables after controlling for all individual and school level factors. Students in high school music ensembles were more likely to have higher standardised mathematics achievement scores, be more concerned about community ethics and be more committed to school.

Southgate and Roscigno (2009) using two national data sets, ECLS-K (20,000 US kindergarten students) and NELS:88 (25,000 adolescents) and three measures of music participation in school, outside school and parental involvement in the form of concert attendance found that music involvement varied systematically by class and gender status. Involvement had implications for both mathematics and reading achievement for young children and adolescents and associations between music and achievement persisted even when prior achievement was taken into account. There was evidence of social class variation in within-school music involvement in adolescents but not in early childhood, while the effects of class on parental music involvement were strong and consistent in both samples. Southgate and Roscigno suggested that this was likely to be related to resource issues. As a mediator of educational outcomes music involvement was significant for both mathematics and reading achievement. It generally increased achievement levels although gains were not distributed equally among all students, a white student advantage existed. This may relate to the type of musical activity engaged in and the opportunities afforded the students for performance which may contribute to enhanced self-esteem and increased motivation.

Evidence from El Sistema and Sistema inspired projects has indicated a positive impact of participating in musical activities on attainment. In the UK, where the programme focuses on children in schools in deprived areas, Smithhurst (2011) reported that after one year of participation in the programme children in Years 1-4 in one school were achieving better scores in mathematics, reading and writing compared with their peers who were not involved. Ninety percent of the children were reaching target grades in maths compared with sixty-eight percent not involved in the programme. Similar trends were evident in reading with eighty-five percent of programme children reaching target grades compared with sixty-two percent not in the programme and in writing (sixty-five percent compared with forty-five percent). Burns and Bewick (2011) reported that after two years of participating in the programme where children engaged with music for 4.5 hours per week forty-three percent of the children had progressed more than four levels in maths, fifty-three percent in reading and forty-two percent in writing compared with a national average of three levels, despite the fact that the participants included a high proportion of children with special educational needs. However, the rate of improvement slowed as participation continued. In a programme in Chile, Egaña de Sol (2008) showed a positive effect on academic attainment in verbal and mathematics skills. This was attributed in part to participants holding higher expectations of their academic achievements, although evaluations of other programmes in Chile had mixed results with some programmes having positive results and others no impact (Evaluación de impacto programa orquestas juveniles e infantiles, 2010). Programmes in the USA have indicated increased academic attainment as an outcome of participation with more children achieving roll of honour status particularly where children participated for an extended period of time (Creech et al., 2013). Creech and colleagues (2013) in their review of El Sistema and Sistema inspired programmes concluded:

'with few exceptions the studies demonstrate significant and steady improvement in academic attainment, achieving targets and in some cases outperforming comparison groups in maths, reading and writing. There is some evidence that these effects may be cumulative, related to prolonged engagement in the programmes' (page 67).

There have been a small number of experimental studies on the effects of participation in music on general attainment. Barr and colleagues (2002) and Hoffman (1995) indicated a positive effect. Similarly, Cabanac and colleagues (2013) compared the performance of students who participated in a music programme in a single school in Canada with those who did not and found that the music students had consistently higher attainment. Hines (2000), studying students with learning difficulties from kindergarten through to ninth grade found neither reading nor mathematics achievement was affected by type of music instruction, motoric or non-motoric. Legette (1993) also found no effect of music instruction. Schneider and Klotz (2000) compared the impact of enrolment in music performance classes or athletic extracurricular activities on academic achievement and found that all groups were equivalent in the fifth and sixth grade but during the seventh, eighth and ninth grades the musicians achieved significantly higher academic achievement scores than the athletes but not than non-participant controls.

Overall, the evidence from correlation studies suggests that children who experience musical training have advantages across all school subjects except sport even after general intelligence is controlled for (Wetter et al., 2009). Their performance is better than might be expected based on their scores on intelligence tests (Corrigall et al., 2013; Schellenberg, 2006). However, the relationship may not be causal as more able children may be more attracted than the less able to musical activities, although as overall academic attainment depends on the development of basic literacy skills which do seem to be enhanced through transfer effects from musical activities prior intellectual advantage is not likely to be the only explanation. Motivation is also crucial in how well children perform at school and is closely linked to self-perceptions of ability, self-efficacy and aspirations (Hallam, 2005). If active engagement with music increases positive perceptions of self, this may transfer to other areas of study and increase motivation to persist. A study by the Norwegian Research Council for Science and Humanities supported this finding a connection between having musical competence and high motivation which led to a greater likelihood of success in school (Lillemyr, 1983). There were high correlations between positive self-perception, cognitive competence, self-esteem, and interest and involvement in school music. The extent to which music activities enhance positive self-beliefs may be an important factor in increasing motivation and may also explain the contradictory findings relating to attainment.

Related to this, participating in high quality musical activities seems to affect aspirations which enhance motivation and subsequently attainment. Devroop (2009) explored the effects of music tuition on the career plans of disadvantaged South African youth and found positive outcomes. There is also extensive evidence from El Sistema and Sistema inspired programmes that engagement with music tuition and participation in an orchestra acts to enhance aspirations (see Creech et al., 2013).

Lewis and colleagues (2011) reported raised aspirations in part attributed to contact with inspirational role models. Uy (2010) noted a major positive impact with regard to enhanced academic aspirations with one hundred per cent of students being enrolled in high school, university or conservatoire with forty percent studying music and others pursuing a range of other academic subjects. Galarce and colleagues (2012) reported improved academic aspirations and students less likely to procrastinate in their school work, while Cuesta (2008) found that sixty three percent of participants achieved better in school compared with fifty percent of non-participants. Many of the USA Sistema inspired programmes also identified elevated aspirations as a goal and indicated success in this respect. Overall, Creech and colleagues (2013) concluded that raised aspirations were one of the most frequently cited positive outcomes of Sistema inspired programmes.

Participating in arts activities including music may also enhance attainment through providing opportunities to develop different aspects of learning. Burton and colleagues (1999) described a taxonomy of eight general areas where this may occur including the opportunity to express ideas and emotions, enhanced and focused perception, the opportunity to make connections, to observe layered and complex relationships between diverse forms of knowledge, being able to construct and organise new meanings, to perceive and understand various points of view, to imagine new possibilities, and to provide opportunities for sensory learning. Music students may also be more conscientious than non-music students which may explain why they are more successful at school than would be indicated by their IQ scores (Corrigal et al., 2013).

Overall, the evidence suggests a positive relationship between active music making and general attainment. What underpins this relationship is less clear. The relationship may be mediated by other factors, for instance, transfer of aural, phonemic, spatial and memory skills or those relating to planning, motivation or changed aspirations.

Music and personality

The study of personality in relation to attainment generally and musically specifically is important as it may be a mediating factor in the transfer of skills. Such research as has been undertaken into the personality of musicians has tended to compare musicians with non-musicians or compare the personalities of musicians playing different instruments or working in different genres. Research exploring the personality characteristics of Western classical musicians suggests that they are bold introverts who direct energy inwards and appear outwardly reserved, the nature of solitary practice encouraging autonomy and independence of thought (Kemp 1996).

Differences have been identified between players of different instruments and those working in different genres. String players tend to be introverted, imaginative and radical, while brass players are more extraverted and have lower levels of self-discipline in comparison to other performing groups. Percussionists also tend towards extroversion. These findings suggest that the extent of practice required for these different instruments (typically more for string players) and their role in the orchestra (more prominent for brass, wind and percussion players) either attracts people with personality characteristics suited to these roles or that these characteristics develop in response to the particular demands being made of them by their chosen roles in the music profession (Kemp 1996; Wills & Cooper 1988). More recent research comparing classical and pop/rock musicians in terms of sensation seeking which found higher levels in the pop/rock musicians supports the notion that particular types of music attract those with particular temperaments (Vuust et al., 2010).

One personality facet which is of particular interest in relation to attainment is conscientiousness as this may be a mediating factor in explaining differences between young musicians and non-musicians. There is certainly evidence that undergraduate music students exhibit conscientious-like traits (Kemp, 1996; Marchant-Haycox & Wilson, 1992), although composers and rock musicians are less conscientious than the general population (Gillespie & Myors, 2000; Kemp, 1996). It may be that those who are more self-disciplined are more likely to persevere in learning a musical instrument. Costa-Giomi (2006) observed children for three years as they began, continued and discontinued lessons. Those who completed three years of lessons were more responsible, disciplined and able to concentrate. However, these traits characterized the students before they started to learn an instrument and did not change as a result of music instruction. Another explanation comes from research by Butkovic and colleagues (2015) who found that music specific flow proness was the best predictor of time spent practising when openness to experience, motivation and intelligence were taken into account.

Another strand of research has focused on the extent to which musicians are open to new experiences. The evidence suggests that they tend to be more creative, imaginative and interested in change (Kemp, 1996; Gibson et al., 2009). Research utilising the big-five personality measure (see John et al., 2008) has shown that duration of music training in childhood is associated positively with openness-to-experience, and that this association remains evident when cognitive ability is held constant. In 10-12-year-old children, duration of training is associated with both conscientiousness and openness-to-experience as assessed through self and parental reports (Corrigal et al., 2013). Personality variables are at least as good as cognitive variables at predicting involvement in music training (Corrigall et al., 2013). When children begin to take formal music lessons at around seven or eight years of age, the best predictors of participating in music training are the parent's openness-to-experience and the child's agreeableness (Corrigall & Schellenberg, 2014) suggesting that child compliance with parental wishes may be a factor.

Overall, the evidence suggests that there are links between personality and aspects of musical participation. What is not clear from the existing research is the direction of causality. The issue is whether engagement with music making leads to the development or enhancement of particular personality characteristics or whether individuals select musical activities which suit their existing characteristics.

Educational motivation and re-engagement of the disaffected

A small number of studies have demonstrated that engagement with music is related to positive attitudes towards school and better attendance (Davalos et al., 1999; Eccles & Barber, 1999; Taetle, 1999; Miszak, 2010). A review of El Sistema and Sistema inspired programmes concluded that one of the most positive outcomes was positive attitudes towards school (Creech et al., 2013). School attendance tended to improve with participation but as most of the programmes commenced at primary level where attendance tends to be good anyway the evidence relating to this was inconclusive (Creech et al., 2013).

One strand of research has focused on the possible role of music education in re-engaging disaffected learners. For instance, in a case study of a general music class in a Spanish public secondary school undertaken with disaffected learners who had received a total of 130 reprimands throughout the school year for poor behaviour and systematically rejecting school rules, Rusinek (2008) established that they enjoyed their music lessons. This may have been because the music teacher generated enthusiasm through an inclusive pedagogy in which the principle of music for all was adopted. Arrangements for percussion instruments, in four to twelve parts, of pop, classical and film music were played by each class. The goal of performance was shared by children and the teacher and was widely accepted as an important part of school culture. Similarly, an Australian study showed that a group of boys who were identified with behavioural issues who engaged in a proactive music making activity showed notable improvements in both classroom cooperation and self-esteem. The drumming exercises in the program were among the most popular and connected closely to the participants' sense of maleness. The activities were fun and provided opportunities for students to enhance positive values such as group cohesion and self-esteem along with their behavioural and social competence (Smith, 2001).

Drumming seems to be a particularly effective form of musical intervention when children are disaffected (Bittman et al., 2001). It can support anger management, team building and substance abuse recovery leading to an increase in self-esteem and the development of leadership skills (Mikenas, 2003). Group drumming can foster a sense of cohesion as it teaches co-ordination and team work with participants having to assume different roles and work together (Drake, 2003). Faulkner and colleagues (2012) developed a drumming programme as a way of engaging at-risk youth, while simultaneously incorporating themes and discussions relating to healthy relationships with others. An evaluation of the programme with a sample of 60 participants in Western Australia's Wheatbelt region using quantitative and qualitative methods, including informal discussions with staff and participants, observation, participant and teacher questionnaires, and school attendance and behavioural incident records showed an increase in scores on a range of social indicators that demonstrated connection with the school community.

In the UK, one strand of research has focused on young people who are not in education, employment or training (NEETs). For instance, one study examined the impact on 48 children and young people who had engaged in a singing programme, Sing Up (Hampshire & Matthijsse, 2010). The findings indicated that participants' self-confidence and aspirations were enhanced and that they developed new peer friendships and connections with parents. However, Hampshire and Matthijsse cautioned that children and young people from privileged backgrounds benefitted more than those from disadvantaged backgrounds, as they risked rejection by their existing friends as the program was perceived as "cheesy" or "gay". This indicates the importance of any musical intervention being seen as relevant to the participants. A review of 15 Youth Music Funded projects (Qa Research, 2012) showed a range of positive outcomes associated with engaging NEETs or those at-risk in music making activity. Outcomes included increased motivation to engage in education, employment, or voluntary activity including gaining qualifications, heightened aspirations, and a more positive attitude towards learning. Participants also developed a range of transferable skills including basic academic skills, listening, reasoning and decision making, concentration / focus, team working, time keeping, goal setting and meeting deadlines. There was also evidence of enhanced well-being including increased self-esteem, self-respect, pride, empowerment, sense of achievement and confidence and an expansion of friendships, trust and improved relationships with adults. Aggression, hyperactivity and impulsivity decreased as participants learned to control their emotions. The projects also broadened horizons including increased awareness of different cultures and traditions.

An evaluation of the European Social Fund project, Engaging Disaffected Young People (LLSC, 2003) found that music and sport activities could encourage participants back in to learning by changing negative attitudes and perceptions towards education, Following completion of the project, eighty-five per cent of the 173 project participants were working towards a qualification. Alvaro and colleagues (2010) evaluated the pilot phase of the European Union's E-Motion Project which was designed to utilise youth friendly music software in order to engage 14-17 year olds who had 'dropped out' of school, or who were at-risk of 'dropping out'. Three experimental pilot programmes were delivered to groups containing between 19 and 26 students in single schools in three different countries: Italy, Romania and the UK. Teachers completed a score card for each student at the beginning and end of each programme. Overall, there were improvements in a range of basic academic skills and personal skills including listening and speaking, and alcohol avoidance. Interviews also indicated a reduction in offending, anti-social behaviour and substance abuse and for some participants enhanced interest in schoolwork, improved school attendance, attention, self-confidence, self-belief, motivation, cultural awareness and communication skills.

Some research has focused on whether engaging in making music can be beneficial to those young people in custody in the juvenile criminal justice system. In the USA, Baker and Homan (2007) studied the implementation of a music programme including piano, guitar, rapping, and computer based music sequencing and composition for a group of pre-dominantly black youths within a detention centre offering a highly practical and direct means of allowing youth offenders to express a particular form of creativity in connection with their existing music and cultural interests. The treatment centre where the programme was based dealt primarily with anger management and substance abuse problems. Young people remained in the facility for an average of 90 days and only those with good behaviour were allowed to participate in the musical activities. Lessons were conducted with individuals or in small groups. While there were many benefits of the programme there were considerable challenges including time pressure, access to lessons which depended on the accumulation of privileges, lack of opportunities for practice and lack of opportunities for continuation on release.

In the UK, Anderson and Overy (2010) examined whether music and art classes could engage young offenders in ongoing education. Fourteen young offenders in Scotland voluntarily participated in the ten-week study. Participants were divided into three groups: music, art and a control education group. They completed pre- and post-interviews and measures that examined their emotions, self-esteem, self-control and literacy skills. Behavioural reports and enrolment in education courses were reviewed for three months before and after the project. The findings indicated increased engagement with education during and after the project for individuals in the music and art groups. Also in the UK, De Viggiani (2014) carried out a three year research project with 118 young people from 19 youth justice programmes. Each music programme had up to ten participants and ran for six half days each lasting from one and a half to three hours. The approach was active and participatory and included singing, word association, lyrics, artwork, work with live instruments, music composition, and the production of a CD or the giving of a live performance. Most of the volunteers identified with the music as being familiar and safe. For some it brought credibility and celebrity success with peers but also the expression of criminal identity (genres associated with drugs, guns, gangs, misogyny). As in the study by Baker and Homan (2007), there were a great many challenges for the tutors in implementing the program including the highly varied demographics of participants, the transience of the offender population, drop out, lack of opportunities for follow up, dependence on gate keepers, difficult group dynamics, lack of decision making skills in participants and passivity or resistance as a self-preservation strategy. Despite this the program showed the potential to support young people in coping with difficult circumstances and for some delivering life-changing benefits.

In research on a Sistema inspired program, Castaneda-Castaneda (2009) working in Columbia explored the impact on young people in a youth detention centre. Intensive guitar workshops were offered as part of a rehabilitation programme and were argued to have developed musical and citizenships skills. Article author query

In South Africa, Woodward and colleagues (2008) evaluated instruction in African marimba and djembe ensemble performance on the behaviour of juvenile offenders. The programme integrated music teaching, mentoring and intercultural exchanges aimed at both the acquisition of musical skills that offered opportunities for diversion from crime and at successful reintegration into society. The children made rapid progress in developing musical skills. Interviews with parents revealed that family relationships improved and students were more co-operative and helpful, demonstrating respect and acting responsibly. There were also positive outcomes in terms of attitudes towards school. The reoffending rate for the pilot group in the six months post-program was nine percent, while in the second six months, this dropped to zero, with no repeat offences committed (Mathiti, 2002). The program was successful in aiding the children to connect with their families, communities, and culture.

In the USA, Tyson (2002) studied the effects of Hip Hop Therapy on self-concept and peer relations in a residential setting for at-risk youth. The program comprised hip-hop, bibliotherapy and music therapy that involved discussion of rap lyrics, emphasising positive themes including identity, peace and unity. Participants spoke highly of the project although there were no statistically significant changes in quantitative measures of outcomes. Similar mixed findings were reported by Gann

(2010) who assessed the effects of music on self-concept and peer support in a small sample of at-risk pupils from two urban schools.

A systematic review of research on the impact of active music making on young people at-risk within the criminal justice system in the UK, Australia, the USA, Canada and South Africa undertaken by Daykin and colleagues (2011) showed that music offered the potential for improvements in self-efficacy, self-esteem and self-concept (Anderson and Overy, 2010; Bittman et al., 2009; Kennedy, 1998; Tyson, 2002) with some participants showing improvements in mood, reduced anger, increased motivation and improved behaviour (Anderson and Overy, 2010; Bittman et al., 2009; Woodward et al., 2008). Overall, the review concluded that music projects could help in positive identity construction (Baker and Homan, 2007; de Roeper and Savelsberg, 2009; Woodward et al., 2008) and could empower young people (Baker and Homan, 2007; de Roeper and Savelsberg, 2009; Lotter, 2003; Woodward et al., 2008). The impact was in part mediated by the extent that the young people had ownership of the music. This varied across contexts and was influenced by a range of factors, including the skills and approaches of those leading the projects (Baker and Homan, 2007; Gann, 2010; Lashua, 2005; Tyson, 2002).

Overall, the evidence suggests that music and arts programmes provide a safe means for young offenders to express difficult emotions and anger, although very short projects where participants are unable to meet their goals can lead to frustration (de Roeper and Savelsberg, 2009). Positive outcomes for music interventions have also been reported with adult offenders (Eastburn, 2003; Digard et al. 2007; Henley et al., 2012). In these studies participants enhanced their communication and social skills, increased their confidence, were better able to reflect on their situation and believed that they could change and attain their goals. There is also evidence that after participation in such projects prisoners seek out opportunities for further education and training (Wilson & Logan, 2006).

Taken together, the evidence suggests that music can be a vehicle for re-engaging young people in education and supporting those who are at-risk in making changes in their lives. The context within which the projects operate is important in their success as are the musical genres focused on and the quality of the musical facilitators. Deane and colleagues (2011) in an interview study of music mentors found that whilst music making acted as a 'hook' in terms of initial project engagement, it was frequently the building of a trusting and non-judgemental relationship between a young person and their mentor that supported change.

Social cohesion and inclusion

Several theories have focused on music's importance in relation to social cohesion. Sloboda (1985) has speculated that music making is 'rewarding' because participating in it generates social bonding and cultural coherence. Its role in a range of ceremonies supports this view (Roederer, 1984). Its survival value lies in synchronising the mood of many individuals who can then collectively take action to strengthen their means of protection and defend themselves from attack (Dowling & Harwood, 1986). Moving together rhythmically in music and dance may reinforce this process (Kogan, 1997). This theoretical approach suggests that music reinforces 'groupishness', the formation and maintenance of group identity, collective thinking, synchronisation and catharsis (the collective expression and experience of emotion) (Brown, 1991), assisting in the forming of coalitions, the promotion of co-operative behaviour and the creating of potential for hostility towards out groups. Cross (2003) takes these arguments further. Drawing on the work of Smith and Szathmary (1995), who maintain that human culture constitutes one of the main transitions in evolution, and the work of Mithen (1996) that suggests that the appearance of homo sapiens is marked by the emergence of a flexible cross-domain cognitive capacity, he argues that:

'music is uniquely fitted to have played a significant role in facilitating the acquisition and maintenance of the skill of being a member of a culture – of interacting socially with others - as well as providing a vehicle for integrating our domain-specific competences so as to endow us with the multi-purpose and adaptive cognitive capacities which make us human.' (2003:52)

Support for the importance of group music making in relation to social cohesion comes from research by Hove and Risen (2009) who have demonstrated how short term exposure to music and tapping in synchrony is able to create social cohesion and increased affiliation. Similar findings have emerged from research with fourteen month old infants who were bounced either in synchrony with the experimenter they were facing or at a faster or slower tempo. Those bounced in synchrony were subsequently more likely to help the experimenter when she dropped objects which were needed to complete a task than those bounced out of synchrony. Experiencing musical rhythms with others seems to be important for social development in infants and promoting social bonding between infants and their caregivers (Trainor, 2014). The pleasure of performing in temporal synchrony with others is also likely to have wide-ranging consequences for wellbeing and overall functioning (McNeill, 1995).

Group music-making involves a strong 'element of sociability' (Finnegan, 1989: 328) and the links between music and social bonding (Cross, 2009; Hagen & Bryant, 2003) and music and emotion (Juslin & Sloboda, 2001) may contribute to explaining why group music making enhances perceived wellbeing.

Some research has been undertaken exploring the impact of active music making on social cohesion in schools. Early research in Switzerland showed that increasing the amount of classroom music within the curriculum did not have a detrimental effect on language and reading skills despite a reduction in time in these lessons (Spychiger, et al., 1993; Zulauf, 1993) and there was an increase in social cohesion within class, greater self-reliance, better social adjustment and more positive attitudes in the children. These effects were particularly marked in low ability, disaffected pupils (Spychiger et al., 1993).

More recently, Eerola and Eerola (2013) tested whether music education could create social benefits within the school environment in Finland. The quality of school life was assessed with 735 participating pupils some of whom were engaged in extended music classes commencing at age nine. Inclusion in the classes was selective with children having to sing a solo and repeat rhythmic and melodic patterns in order to be accepted. Once in the classes the children had an average of three extra music lessons per week (about four hours compared with 1.4 hours). The impact of the extended musical classes was assessed when the children were in Year 3 (baseline) and Year 6. A standardised self-assessment measure of Quality of School Life (Linnakyla & Malin, 1997) containing 29 items including general satisfaction with school, teacher student relations, status in class, identity in class, achievement and opportunity, and negative affect was used. Five items were added to assess classroom climate. While most measures were the same in Year 3 the extended music group had higher attainment scores for maths and Finnish language and literature. By Year 6 the extended music groups had higher scores for climate in the classroom, were generally more satisfied with school life, had a sense of achievement and felt they had opportunities. These outcomes may have occurred as a result of attending a class where others shared an interest, through the appreciation by others of public performances, the experience of intense emotional experiences from music, feelings of affiliation and the pro-social effects of joint musical activities.

Group music making may also contribute to feelings of social inclusion (Minguella & Buchanan, 2009). In a national study of 2000 children in the UK those who were relatively more skilled and developed in their musical understanding and performance were also statistically highly likely to report themselves as being more socially included (Welch et al., 2009). Rinta and colleagues (2011) explored the connections between children's musical backgrounds and their feelings of social inclusion in the UK and Finland. One hundred and ten 8-11 year old children participated in the research. The children felt more socially included when they played a musical instrument or sang with their friends. Statistically significant connections were found between the regularity of group music making and singing activities and feelings of social inclusion. The more frequent the engagement in social musical activities the more socially included the children felt. Other research has indicated that music festivals with students performing to the public can be used to promote feelings of social inclusion and reduce absenteeism in Roma children (Almau, 2005), while folksongs have been used in Israel to bring Palestinian and Jewish children and their families together during cross-community school visits (Lichman, 2006; Lichman & Sullivan, 2000).

One strand of research has explored how group music making can support the social inclusion of refugee children. In an Australian school catering for newly arrived immigrants, music has been used to support acculturation and integration (Marsh, 2012a, 2012b). The children aged 12-18 participated in musical activities designed to provide opportunities for cultural maintenance, cross-cultural transmission and verbal and nonverbal communication with a view to developing interpersonal connections, social cohesion and student empowerment through varied learning, teaching, and performance opportunities. One area which emerged as important in achieving these outcomes was the participation in performance in a major school concert. Key outcomes for students included feelings of belonging to the school community, the wider Australian community, as well as to a global music community disseminated through various technological media (Marsh, 2012a, 2012b).

Group music making also offers the opportunity to engage in wider cultural experiences, explore new ideas, places and perspectives and support social cohesion through broadening experience (Israel, 2012). These not only benefit participants but also increase parents' attendance at cultural events and their exposure to culture more generally (Creech et al., 2013).

Participating in group music making can encourage tolerance and the development of social ethics, for instance, there is evidence that music participation can increase acceptance of children with intellectual impairments (Humpal, 1991; Jellison et al., 1984). Concern with wider community issues may also be enhanced. Miszka (2010) investigated the relationships between participation in a range of musical ensembles and community ethics in a very large sample of pupils in over 600 schools. Music participation was related to community ethics including having strong friendships, helping people in the community and working to correct social and economic inequalities. Wiltermutt and Heath (2009) showed that students in the USA scored higher on a weak-linked co-ordination exercise and a public good game after singing along with a song played on headphones compared to no singing or forced asynchronous singing.

Group music making clearly has the potential to promote social cohesion and support inclusion. Making music with others creates bonds which are not easily created in other ways. This process may also lead participating individuals to become more tolerant and accepting of others and increase their beliefs in social ethics.

Pro-social behaviour and team work

One of the most frequently cited benefits of group music making is its impact on pro-social behaviour. From an evolutionary perspective, Hagen and Bryant (2003) have argued that group music making and dancing evolved as group displays signalling intentional stability in the group's ability to act collectively establishing meaningful relationships between groups. Huron (2001; 2003) has also suggested that music and dance act as effective tools to establish and maintain social bonds and pro-social commitment among members of social groups increasing cooperation and pro-social behaviour. In the El Sistema programme intensive ensemble activities are seen as a rich opportunity for nurturing positive citizenship skills, including 'respect, equality, sharing, cohesion, team work, and, above all, the enhancement of listening as a major constituent of understanding and cooperation' (Majno, 2012, p. 58).

There is evidence of the impact of active group music making on pro-social behaviour in young children. For instance, Kirschner and Tomasello (2009; 2010) studied four year olds in tasks requiring identical skills in musical and non-musical conditions. Joint music making enhanced cooperation and helpful behaviour. The research also showed the importance of working with others in developing musical skills. The children were better able to drum along to a beat when the drum was played by an instructor than when it was played mechanically or they were exposed to an audio recording only.

The El Sistema programme and projects inspired by it where children experience intensive and prolonged engagement in an orchestral community facilitate pro-social behaviour. Slevin and Slevin (2013) suggest that El Sistema and Sistema inspired programmes offer a safe and nurturing space where children learn what it means to pursue an ideal. They argue that this team work where the goal depends on individual effort enables personal development. Similarly, Lewis and colleagues (2011) revealed improvements in social skills and the development of positive group identity in a Sistema inspired programme. Pupil surveys administered two years apart indicated statistically significant change in relation to social skills and relationships. Children reported how they tried to help others and take turns. Interviews with parents and teachers reinforced these findings. In Ireland, after three years, a Sistema inspired programme was found to foster a strong positive group identity. When asked to design a new school crest every child produced a design that included a musical symbol (Kenny & Moore, 2011). Parents and others in evaluations by Campe and Kaufman (2013) and Savoie (2012) indicated that playing in Sistema inspired musical groups supported students in their social development providing an important scaffold for developing collaborative skills. These skills transferred to other school and home settings. Many of the evaluations of Sistema inspired programmes in the USA also refer to enhanced peer relationships, demonstrating respect and having consideration for others. Because of their experiences in orchestras and ensembles participants understood the importance of working co-operatively (see Creech et al., 2013). Galarce and colleagues (2012) based on findings from focus group data found that students participating in a Sistema inspired programme in the Caribbean demonstrated improved social skills, cooperation, team work, communication and a protective social network after only six months of participation. Quantitative data showed that students were significantly less likely to get angry and be aggressive and be less involved in teasing, shoving, hitting, kicking or fighting. Similarly, Bergerson and Motto (2013) found that students experienced greater empathy for students who shared their interests. This was supported by evidence from other El Sistema and Sistema inspired programmes (see Creech et al., 2013) although there were exceptions. For instance, Villalba (2010) found that some students did not feel completely integrated and others were bored. This suggests that the nature of the musical activities plays an important role in mediating any wider non-musical outcomes.

Research in the USA has shown that involvement in group music activities in the high school helps individuals learn to support each other, maintain commitment and bond together for group goals (Sward, 1989). The benefits of band participation have been reported to include accomplishment, appreciation, discipline, fun, active participation and maturing relationships (Brown, 1980). Ninety-five per cent of parents of non-band participants believed that band provided educational benefits not found in other classrooms and seventy-eight per cent agreed that band was more educational than extra-curricular. Band directors talked in general terms about the benefits of discipline, teamwork, co-ordination, development of skills, pride, lifetime skills, accomplishment, cooperation, sense of belonging, responsibility, self-expression, creativity, performance, companionship, building character and personality, social development and enjoyment

In the UK, peripatetic instrumental teachers working in schools have reported considerable benefits of learning to play an instrument including the development of social skills; gaining a love and enjoyment of music; developing team-work; developing a sense of achievement, confidence and self-discipline; and developing physical co-ordination (Hallam and Prince, 2000). Being involved in the extra-curricular re-hearsal and performance of a school show has been shown to facilitate the development of friendships with like-minded individuals and make a contribution to social life through a widespread awareness of the show by non-participants (Pitts, 2007). Such participation increased pupils' confidence, social networks and sense of belonging, despite the time commitment which inevitably impinged on other activities. Reflecting on previous and current group music making activities, university music students have reported benefits in terms of pride in being an active con-tributor to a group outcome, developing a strong sense of belonging, gaining popularity and making friends with 'like-minded' people, and the enhancement of social skills (Kokosaki & Hallam, 2007; 2011). A study of 84 members of a college choral society showed that eighty-seven per cent believed that they had benefitted socially, seventy-five per cent emotionally, and forty-nine per cent spiritually. Meeting new peo-ple, feeling more positive, and being uplifted spiritually were all referred to (Clift & Hancox, 2001).

Several studies have focused on promoting pro-social behaviour in adults. Working in musical groups has been found to promote feelings of belonging, social adjustment, trust and co-operation among co-workers. Anshel and Kipper (1988) found that adult Israeli males co-operated better in a prisoner dilemma game and scored higher on questionnaire of trust after a group singing lesson compared to passive music listening and other non-musical activities. In Northern Ireland, Odena (2010) studied the perceptions of 14 key practitioners engaged in musical activi-ties in cross community settings working with protestant and catholic groups. The interview data showed that cross community music educa-tion projects were an effective means of addressing prejudice amongst young people. However, the specific contexts of each setting can set limits on what can be achieved.

Within small musical groups social relationships and the development of trust and respect are crucial for their functioning (Davidson & Good, 2002; Davidson & King, 2004; Goodman, 2000; Young & Colman, 1979). For long-term success rehearsals have to be underpinned by strong social frameworks as interactions are typically characterised by conflict and compromise related mainly to musical content and its co-ordination, although some interactions are of a more personal nature (e.g. approval) (Murningham & Conlon, 1991; Young & Colman, 1979); the smaller the group the more important personal friendship seems to be.

Making music with others in small and large groups requires team work, particularly when music is to be performed. Team work relies on participating individuals supporting each other and developing trust and respect. Group music making provides an ideal vehicle for developing pro-social, team working skills.

Empathy and emotional intelligence

Members of musical groups have to pay attention to the actions and intentions of the other players and their physical and emotional states (Cross et al., 2012). This promotes states of togetherness (Huron, 2001; 2003; Cross, 2009). Understanding the emotional state of others is key to developing empathy, the ability to produce appropriate responses to the situation of others that approximate their responses and experiences as well as an awareness and identification of their emotions (Lieberman, 2007). Cross and colleagues (2012) suggest that there are empathy-promoting musical components which can lead to shared intentionality and understanding of others' intentions, the adoption of a common object of attention (Tomasello et al., 2005) and to intersubjectivity (Rabinowitch et al., 2012).

There is some evidence for the development of increased empathy in children through musical participation. Hietolahtiansten and Kalliopuska (1990) surveyed 12 year old children who had been musically active for about six years and same-age control children with no musical activity and found that the musically trained children scored significantly higher on scores of empathy. Pre-school and primary school children who participated in a special music-empathy programme that highlighted the importance of empathy through singing and composing songs about empathy as well as discussing how children empathise also demonstrated high empathy levels (Kalliopuska & Ruokonen, 1986; 1993; Kalliopuska & Tiitinen, 1991). Rabinowitch and colleagues (2013) studied 52 children aged 8-11 years who were randomly assigned to musical activities, games or acted as a control group. The musical intervention consisted of a range of musical games which were designed to encourage musical interactions and working together creatively. Entrainment games were designed to encourage rhythmic coordination, and imitation games to highlight imitative and gestural encounters, shared intentionality and inter-subjectivity. The children took a battery of tests at the beginning and end of the study which included three measures of emotional empathy. Two out of three of the empathy measures increased in the music group children.

Related to empathy is the concept of emotional sensitivity. As music is closely linked with the emotions it is possible that active music making may have the capacity to increase emotional sensitivity (Hunter and

Schellenberg 2010). For instance, Resnicow and colleagues (2004) found that there was a relationship between the ability to recognise emotions in performances of classical piano music and measures of emotional intelligence which required individuals to identify, understand, reason with and manage emotions using hypothetical scenarios. The two were significantly correlated which suggests that identification of emotion in music performance draws on some of the same skills that make up everyday emotional intelligence. There is also evidence that music training enhances sensitivity to emotions in speech (Thompson et al., 2004). Similarly, Schellenberg and Mankarious (2012) studied the relationship between understanding emotions and music training in 60 7-8 year olds. The musically trained children had at least eight months of formal training out of school mainly through private individual lessons. The findings showed a positive association between music training and emotional ability, although this seemed to be mediated by higher levels of general intelligence.

Some of the research exploring the relationships between music making and emotional intelligence has had mixed findings. This seems to depend on whether emotional intelligence is being measured as a trait (a behavioural disposition) or as an ability (skill in processing emotional information and using it in everyday life). Music training seems to be more related to emotional intelligence as a trait (Petrides et al., 2006) rather than an ability (Trimmer & Cuddy, 2008; Schellenberg, 2011b). For instance, Schellenberg (2011b) studied 196 undergraduates ranging in age from 17-26 years with at least eight years of extracurricular private music lessons or no lessons. The musically trained participants had higher scores on measures of intelligence than their untrained counterparts but this did not extend to an ability based measure of emotional intelligence.

The evidence suggests that group music making can support the development of empathy and emotional intelligence although the evidence relating to the latter is less clear. This is in part because emotional intelligence is a contested concept. While music seems to be related to trait emotional intelligence which is conceptualised as an element of personality (Petrides & Furnham, 2001) it does not seem to have a relationship with the process conception where it is viewed as being able to perceive, understand, process and regulate emotional information (Salovey & Mayer, 2004).

Psychological well-being

The benefits of active engagement with music in relation to psychological well-being across the lifespan are well documented (Rickard & McFerran, 2012). Positive associations between music engagement and health and well-being are evident in adolescents (e.g. Miranda & Gaudreau, 2011), adults (e.g. Greasley and Lamont, 2006; Saarikallio, 2011) and the elderly (e.g. Creech et al., 2014; Hallam et al., 2014; Hays & Mininchiello, 2005; Laukka, 2007). Music is increasingly being recognised for its beneficial effects on physical health and wellbeing (Hanser, 2010; MacDonald et al, 2012; Pelletier, 2004).

Since the 1980s a considerable body of research has demonstrated the relationship between music-making and subjective wellbeing (Clift et al., 2010; Lehmberg & Fung, 2010). In addition to encouraging social participation, group singing has been found to reduce anxiety and depression (Houston et al., 1998; Lally, 2009; Sandgren, 2009; Wise et al., 1992; Zanini & Leao, 2006). People from a range of different backgrounds can experience benefits to their emotional and physical well-being from making music with an increased sense of self-worth and enhanced social skills and wider social networks (Bailey & Davidson, 2002; 2003; 2004).

Babies born premature or underweight can benefit from the stimulation of music (Caine, 1991; Cassidy & Standley, 1995). Music can significantly reduce the frequency and duration of episodes of inconsolable crying as well as lead to improvement in physiological measures including heart rate, respiration rate, oxygen saturation and mean arterial pressure (Keith et al., 2009; Loewy, 2014). When entrained with a premature infant's observed vital signs, sound and lullabies can improve feeding behaviours and sucking patterns and increase prolonged periods of quiet alert states. Music therapy with hospitalized infants has also shown robust results in relation to infants' capacity to self-regulate and engage in social interaction with adults compared to infants in a control group with no music therapy (Malloch et al., 2012). Music can also be used to promote well-being in healthy six-month old infants (Trehub, 2014).

One strand of research has explored the potential benefits of engagement with music on wellbeing within the family, particularly in young children, where musicality has been argued to be intrinsic to communication between parents and infants (Malloch & Tervarthen, 2009). Parents have been found to use music to support other activities and to create a calm and soothing environment prior to sleep times in addition to participating in child-centred musical activities (Lamont, 2008). Parent-child music therapy efficacy studies indicate that joint active music participation supports improved child-parent interactions and enhances impulse control and self-regulation skills (Pasiali, 2012). Social and communication skills have also been shown to improve with parent-child music therapy (e.g. Mackenzie & Hamlett, 2005; Nicholson et al., 2010; Walworth, 2009) For instance, de Gratzer (1999) in a ten month action research project of group music making between parents and toddlers demonstrated non-verbal communication between parent and child was enhanced. Williams and colleagues (2012) examined the effectiveness of a short-term group music therapy intervention for 201 parents of children with disabilities and explored the factors associated with better outcomes for participating families. Pre- and post-intervention parental questionnaires and clinician observation measures were completed to examine outcomes of parental wellbeing, parenting behaviours, and child development. Significant improvements pre to post intervention were found for parent mental health, child communication and social skills, parenting sensitivity, parental engagement with child and acceptance of child, child responsiveness to parent, and child interest and participation in program activities. There was also evidence for high parental satisfaction and social benefits to families.

Research with disadvantaged children and their parents has also demonstrated benefits of participation in musical activities. For instance, Nicholson and colleagues (2008) explored the effectiveness of a 10-week group music therapy program on 358 parents who were socially disadvantaged, young or had a child with a disability. The children were aged 0-5 years. Musical activities were used to promote positive parent-child relationships and children's behavioural, communicative and social development. Significant improvements were found for therapist-observed parent and child behaviours, parent-reported irritable parenting, educational activities in the home, parent mental health, child communication and social play skills.

El Sistema programmes and those inspired by El Sistema prioritise the psychological and physical well-being of their students. It is therefore perhaps not surprising that evaluations show that the programmes offer a safe and structured environment which ensures that children are occupied and at reduced risk of participating in less desirable activities (Creech et al, 2013). Evaluations of individual programmes report strengthening children's sense of individual and group identity, of children taking pride in their accomplishments, of an enhancement in determination and persistence and of children being better able to cope with anger and express their emotions more effectively. Children value their participation as a social activity, a way to enjoy music with others, strengthened friendships with peers, working in teams and acquiring musical skills. In the UK, Lewis and colleagues (2011) showed that participants had enhanced social listening skills and were more settled in school. Parents reported that the children had grown in confidence, had more positive attitudes and their behaviour was better. The parents suggested that this was because the children were proud of their musical achievements and because the programme offered opportunities for developing social skills and discipline. Teachers also indicated that pupils had a greater sense of purpose and self-confidence. Also in the UK, Smithhurst (2011) and Burns and Berwick (2012) found enhanced confidence, social skills and general wellbeing as outcomes of participation in addition to raised aspirations. Programmes in Scotland and Ireland also showed enhanced confidence, happiness, team working skills, aspirations, self discipline, concentration, focus, engagement with learning and behaviour (GEN, 2011a; 2011b; Kenny and Moore, 2011). Similarly, Wald (2011) researching two Sistema inspired programmes in Argentina found evidence of enhanced self-esteem, self-worth, self-confidence, pride, motivation, commitment, social responsibility and socialisation. Comparing programmes in Venezuela and the USA, Uy (2010) reported improvements in focus, discipline, time management, relaxation and coping, communication, the ability to work with others, academic performance and aspirations, creative thinking and self-esteem. Similar findings were reported for other programmes (for a review see Creech et al., 2013).

Research on the impact of music making on 'looked after children' in the UK has shown that engagement in high quality music-making projects can support the development of resilience in dealing with the challenges that they face. In a review of the evidence, Dillon (2010) showed that music-making could contribute to improved negotiation skills and co-operative working; learning to trust peers; developing the capacity for self-expression and a stronger sense of self awareness; increased self-discipline and responsibility; a sense of achievement; feelings of belonging and shared identity; and the opportunity to make friends and develop positive relationships with adults. Music making provided respite from problems and opportunities to have fun. In addition, there was evidence of increased confidence in terms of personal development and the acquisition of a wide range of skills (Dillon, 2010). In Norway, Waaktaar and colleagues (2004) in a study of young people who had experienced serious and /or multiple life stresses found that a music programme was able to enhance resilience in a group of 15 year old males who had behavioural difficulties. Four central characteristics of resilience, positive peer relations, self-efficacy, coherence and creativity were developed by the young men as they produced a music video for public viewing.

Some research has focused on the role that music can play in supporting the healing of those who have been traumatized. Hesser and Heinemann (2010) provide examples of music projects which have supported the social inclusion of refugees and others who have experienced severe trauma. Several authors have documented the benefits of creative musical activity for children who have experienced war (Osborne, 2009; Heidenrich, 2005; Sutton, 2002) as means of developing self-esteem, trust, identity and social cohesion in a range of countries including Bosnia-Herzogovina, Georgia, Sierra Leone, Rwanda and Palestine. These projects have allowed reflection and the expression of feelings. Some projects have also included dance supporting refugees or displaced young people in Sierra Leone, Ghana, and Slovenia, These programmes supported the development of communication, empowered young people, gave them a sense of belonging and relief and supported identity development (Harris, 2007; Jones et al., 2004; Lederach & Lederach, 2010; Pesek, 2009). Zharinova-Sanderson (2004) reported work with traumatised refugees in Berlin at the Centre for the Treatment of torture victims. Music therapy in this context helped young people to use their own cultural music to adjust to their new culture, while performance opportunities allowed audience members to see beyond traumatised refugees to real people. In Sierra Leone, Gonsalves (2010) worked with traumatised young girls who had been forced to fight and serve as spies, soldier-wives, and camp followers. Through song the girls communicated their emotional and material needs, histories, fears and current difficulties. Creative musical interaction supported increased understanding, re-engagement and connections with others and promoted healing empowering the participants.

Overall, there is considerable evidence that actively making music with others can promote psychological well-being. These benefits are apparent in infants, young children through to old age and include those facing particular life challenges.

Personal development and self-beliefs

The beliefs that we hold about ourselves including those related to our identity make a major contribution to our sense of well-being. At any point in time, an individual may hold multiple identities depending on their current social context. Identities constantly evolve as they are challenged and re-constructed based on the feedback that is received from interactions with others. These may be complementary or contradictory. Historically, the term self-concept was used to refer to how individuals perceived and evaluated themselves in different areas of their lives. In the same way that an individual can hold multiple identities, the self-system is made up of a number of self-images including those relating to self-esteem, self-efficacy, ideal selves and possible selves. These are often context or situation specific and develop in interaction with the environment (Hallam, 2009; in press). Active engagement with music can support the development of musical and other identities and can also impact on self-beliefs. Depending on feedback received from others the impact may be positive or negative.

In the UK, Harland (2000) showed that the most frequent overall influences on pupils derived from engagement with the arts in school were related to personal and social development. In music those who played instruments referred to an increase in self-esteem and sense of identity. In the evaluation of a national singing programme involving in the region of 6000 children, Welch (2010) found that those participating had more positive self-concepts than non-participating children. There was a positive linear relationship between singing development and self-concept. University students looking back on their previous musical experiences at school have highlighted the contribution of making music to the development of a strong sense of self-esteem and satisfaction. They reported enhanced personal skills encouraging the development of self-achievement, self-confidence and intrinsic motivation. A further study with non-music students who had previously participated in musical groups established similar benefits with a particular preoccupation with the impact of group music making on the self and personal development (Kokotsaki & Hallam, 2007; 2011).

Research on school band participation in the USA found benefits in terms of self-confidence and self-esteem (Brown, 1980; 1985). Ninety-one per cent of non-band parents, seventy-nine per cent of non-band students, ninety per cent of drop-out band parents and eighty-two per cent of drop out band students agreed that participating in a band built self-esteem, self confidence and a sense of accomplishment. A study by the Norwegian Research Council for Science and Humanities found high correlations between positive self-perception, cognitive competence score, self-esteem, and interest and involvement in school music (Lillemyr, 1983), while Whitwell (1977) argued that creative participation in music improves self-image, self-awareness, and creates positive self-attitudes. Similar findings have been found with urban black middle school students (Marshall, 1978).

Dege and colleagues (2014) undertook a study exploring the relationships between the number of music lessons experienced and a child's academic self-concept. Data were collected from 92 children aged 12-14 with varied musical backgrounds. Multiple regression analyses which took into account socio-economic status, gender, non-musical out of school activities, grade, IQ and months of music lessons showed that music lessons contributed significantly to the prediction of academic self-concept scores and significantly improved the fit of the model. There was a significant positive association between music lessons and academic self-concept even when confounding variables were controlled for.

In an intervention study, Rickard and colleagues (2013) studied the impact on over 350 young children (grades 1 and 3) of Kodaly music classes for the youngest children with instrumental classes (predominantly strings-based) introduced for the older children in comparison with controls. The findings showed that school-based music classes prevented a decline in global self-esteem measures experienced by the control group in both the younger and older cohorts, and in general and academic self-esteem for the older cohort. The data suggested that increasing the frequency and quality of arts-based activities can be beneficial for the self-esteem of primary school-aged children. However, Hartas (2011) found no relation between parent-reported frequency of singing songs and rhymes or playing music at three years and teacher rated performance on social emotional development at 5 years.

There is some evidence that students who participate in musical activities talk more with their parents and teachers and their parents were more likely to talk with friends' parents. Broh (2002) concluded that these social benefits were likely to lead to higher self-esteem in the children in turn leading to increased motivation and self-efficacy.

El Sistema and Sistema inspired programmes have prioritised the personal and social development of participants and many of the evaluations point to the positive impact on self-beliefs (e.g. Esquaea Torres, 2001; 2004; Galarce et al., 2012; Israel, 2012; Uy, 2010). However, Lewis and colleagues (2011) found no significant changes in self-esteem over time, although comparisons of the self-esteem of children in the two participating schools where there were differences at the beginning of the project had disappeared by the time of the second survey. Lower scoring pupils benefitted the most. Lopez and Berrios (2007) showed that El Sistema orchestras were perceived as providing a positive space for self-affirmation and identity formation. Participation was perceived to show openness to new realities and values, tolerance to diversity, the development of personal identity, and self-affirmation. Creech and colleagues (2013) attributed the impact on self-esteem to recognition by participants of their own abilities and these being acknowledged by families and friends.

Some research has focused on interventions with children who are experiencing particular problems. For instance, Choi and colleagues (2010) investigated the effects of group music activities on children exhibiting highly aggressive behaviour. Forty-eight children were allocated to either a music intervention group or a control group. The music intervention group engaged in 50 minutes of musical activities twice weekly for 15 consecutive weeks. By the end of the programme, the music intervention group showed significant reduction in aggression and improvement in self-esteem compared with the control group. Thomas (2014) undertook a qualitative case study of two children with social, emotional and behavioural difficulties, one who exhibited withdrawn behaviour, the other poor behaviour. Intervention music lessons over a period of one year benefitted the children in terms of personal competence (self-regulation, self-confidence, self-esteem), task competence (enjoyment, engagement, motivation), and social competence (collaboration, social connectedness).

Music therapy studies with young autistic children have shown enhanced social verbal and communication skills and emotional development (Dezfoolian et al., 2013; Hillier et al., 2012; Kim et al., 2009; Oldfield, 2006). One project exploring the impact of musical engagement on 35 young people with special educational needs following a summer residential programme found statistically significant increases with a large effect size for self-esteem, emotional well-being, resilience and life satisfaction. Girls seemed to benefit more than boys (NPC, 2012).

A further strand of research has considered whether there are benefits of music participation for children from deprived communities in terms of enhanced self-esteem. The findings are mixed. For instance, Costa-Giomi (2004) randomly assigned 9-year-olds to three years of individual piano lessons or a no-lessons control group. The two groups did not differ in self-esteem at any point in time. In another study of children who received a two year music intervention, the treatment and control groups did not differ in self-esteem at the beginning or end of the study (Portowitz et al., 2009). In these studies the children received individual music instruction and were not engaged in group music making. In contrast, Devroop (2012) investigated the social-emotional impact of group instrumental music instruction on 84 disadvantaged South African students over a period of two years. The findings showed that there were generally increased levels of self-esteem, optimism, happiness and perseverance after participation in an instrumental music programme.

There is mixed evidence regarding the impact of active engagement with music on self-beliefs. This is not surprising as self-belief systems depend on feedback received from others. If feedback about the development of musical skills and performance is positive then self-beliefs will be enhanced. If this is not the case then no enhancement will occur. If feedback is critical then there could be a negative impact.

Music and health

There has been increasing interest recently in the role of music in health in particular in trying to understand the ways that music can impact on wellbeing and physical health and the extent of the possible benefits (for recent reviews on a range of issues see MacDonald et al., 2012). The impact of music on psychological wellbeing and subsequently good health is largely, although not exclusively, through the emotions it evokes which can be wide ranging (for a review see Juslin and Sloboda, 2010). Music seems to elicit emotions and change moods through its stimulation of the autonomic nervous system. Bodily responses related to emotion include changes in dopamine, serotonin, cortisol, endorphin, and oxytocin levels (see van Eck et al., 1996). These can all affect physical health. Results from a range of experimental, observation, and animal studies support this (e.g. Kubzansky, 2009). In addition to the impact that music can have on emotions it has also long been know that listening to music has a wide range of physiological effects on the human body including changes in heart rate, respiration, blood pressure, skin conductivity, skin temperature, muscle tension, and biochemical responses (see Kreutz & Lotze, 2008).

Music has a particular role in the reduction of stress and anxiety and related to this the reduction of pain and the strengthening of the immune system. Significant reductions in cortisol levels, a psychophysiological measure of stress have been found in healthy adults listening to particular kinds of music (Fukui & Yamashita, 2003; Kreutz et al., 2004; Mockel et al., 1994) when actively making music (Beck et al., 2000) and in clinical contexts (e.g. Le Roux et al., 2007; Spintge, 2012). Music listening can reduce the amount of sedative drugs required in hospital (Conrad et al., 2007) and support recovery after surgery also reducing the need for pain relief medication (Nelson et al., 2008; Spintge & Droh, 1992; Spintge, 2012; Vollert et al., 2003).

Making or listening to music may also impact on the immune system (e.g. Beck et al., 2000; Kuhn, 2002; Kreutz et al., 2004; Beck et al., 2006), can play a therapeutic role in supporting improvement in speech impairments (Pilon et al., 1998; Thaut et al., 2001), support rehabilitation of motor movements (LaGasse & Thaut, 2012) and improve the quality, range, and speed of movements (Schneider et al., 2007).

There also seem to be some general health benefits of participating in making music for older people including lower mortality rates (Byrgen et al., 1996; Hyyppa and Maki, 2001; Konlann et al. ,2000; Johansson et al, 2001), a lack of deterioration in physical health (Hillman, 2002; Cohen et al., 2006; 2007) with fewer visits to the doctor and less use of medication. Music making also contributes to perceived good health, quality of life, and mental well-being (Coffman and Adamek, 1999; Kahn, 1998; Vanderark et al., 1983; Wise et al., 1992), while playing the piano exercises the heart as much as a brisk walk (Parr, 1985).

Early reviews of the research with adult singers have concluded that there can be a range of health and well-being benefits of participating in a choir (Clift et al., 2008; Stacey et al., 2002), although subsequent reviews are more cautious (see Clift, 2012). Perceived benefits include physical relaxation and release of physical tension; emotional release and reduction of feelings of stress; a sense of happiness, positive mood, joy, elation, and feeling high; a sense of greater personal, emotional and physical well-being; an increased sense of arousal and energy; stimulation of cognitive capacities – attention, concentration, memory and learning; an increased sense of self-confidence and self-esteem; a sense of therapeutic benefit in relation to long-standing psychological and social problems; a sense of exercising systems of the body through the physical exertion involved, especially the lungs; a sense of disciplining the skeletal-muscular system through the adoption of good posture; being engaged in a valued , meaningful worthwhile activity that gives a sense of purpose and motivation. There is every reason to suppose that these benefits would also apply to children.

Some research has focused on the impact of active engagement with music on children who are hospitalised (for reviews see Klassen et al., 2008; Preti, 2013; Preti & McFerran, 2014). Commonly, music in paediatric settings is used to enhance the wellbeing of young patients. Children and young people benefit in terms of enhanced relaxation (Malone, 1996; Daveson, 2001; Longhi & Pickett, 2008), providing distraction (Robb, 2003; Caprilli et al., 2007; Hendon & Bohon, 2008) and helping them to talk about the hospital experience and develop coping strategies (Froehlich 1984; Brodsky, 1989; Robb, 2000; 2003). Familiar music can reduce anxiety associated with the hospital environment (Preti and Welch, 2011) and can reduce children's stress during painful procedures (Vohra & Nilsson, 2011; Nguyen et al., 2010; Caprilli et al., 2007; Whitehead-Pleaux et al., 2006; Klassen et al., 2008). In some cases music making can reduce or remove the need for sedation (DeLoach Walworth, 2005). Patients react better to music therapy than other therapies (Hendon & Bohon, 2008; Longhi & Pickett, 2008; Longhi et al., 2013). This may be because music therapy is often perceived as fun

(O'Callaghan et al., 2013a; 2013b). There are also benefits to the families of children in hospital. Parents value being able to participate in musical activities with their child so they can share the experience and open up communication between family members (Lindenfelser et al., 2012). In addition to supporting children during stressful procedures parents are indirectly supported by music creating a more relaxed environment (Preti & Welch, 2004; 2011). There are also benefits for teenagers in participating in music based group programs within hospitals (Bittman et al., 2001; Burns et al., 2005; Nicholson et al., 2008).

Physical development

There is relatively little research exploring the impact of active engagement with making music on physical development despite the fact that children and adults frequently respond to music with movement. For instance, Overy (2014) studied the impact of beat on children's natural responses to music and showed that four year old children showed spontaneous, energetic movement responses of highly periodic, repetitive movement patterns such as jumping swaying and twisting often in close synchrony to the auditory beat pattern, although not always in time. She concluded that the human motor system responds powerfully to an auditory beat pattern but there are large individual differences in preferred movements.

Research in the field of neuroscience has shown that extensive instrumental music training affects the anatomy of the brain with greater gray matter volumes in motor-related areas (Elbert et al., 1995; Hyde et al., 2009; Pascual-Leone, 2001) and greater white matter volumes in motor tracts (Bengtsson et al., 2005) with differences emerging after one year of music training (Hyde et al., 2009; Schlaug et al., 2005). There are also very specific differences in relation to the instruments played (Bangert and Schlaug, 2006). Despite this there is very little evidence of whether these changes in the brain transfer to other physical activities, although there is evidence in general that learning to play an instrument improves fine motor skills (Schlaug et al., 2005). Early training may be important as Watanabe and colleagues (2007) showed that musicians who trained before the age of 7 had better performance in a timed motor sequence task than musicians who began training later.

Research has established that using rhythmic accompaniment to support physical education programmes can improve performance. Anshel and Marisi (1978) observed positive results in performance accuracy and endurance when music was rhythmically synchronised with motor performance. Painter (1966) found similar results. Beisman (1967) found that throwing, catching, jumping and leaping improved when children participated in a programme involving rhythm, while Brown and colleagues (1981) also found that an integrated music and physical education programme improved pre-schoolers motor performance more than movement exploration. Orsmond and Miller (1999) found improved visual-motor skills in pre-school children taking music lessons when compared with controls. Derri and colleagues (2001) investigated the effect of a ten week music and movement programme on the quality of locomotor performance in children of 4-6 years and found that the experimental group improved on galloping, leaping, horizontal jump and skipping. A further study showed that the programme compared favourably with free play activities (Deli et al., 2006).

Conclusions

This synthesis of research findings has indicated that there can be many benefits of active engagement in making music. Some of these benefits have a direct relationship with musical activity. These include those relating to:

- aural perception, which in turn supports the development of language and literacy skills;
- enhanced verbal and visual memory skills;
- spatial reasoning which contributes to some elements of mathematics and constitutes part of measured intelligence;
- executive functioning which is implicated in intelligence and academic learning more generally;
- self-regulation which is implicated in all forms of learning requiring extensive practice;
- creativity, particularly where the musical activities are themselves creative; and
- academic attainment.

Currently, the nature of the specific types of musical activity which are implicated in bringing about particular changes are not clear. For instance, research has shown that there are differences in the brains of those playing different instruments (e.g. Bangert & Schlaug, 2006; Pantev et al., 2001). There is also the issue of the quality of the teaching. When the teaching is poor there may be no benefits and even negative outcomes (Rauscher, 2005).

The age of commencement of training may be an important factor. Some neurological changes may only occur if training starts early, in some cases before the age of seven (Amunts et al., 1997; Elbert et al., 1995; Lee et al., 2003; Li et al., 2010; Musacchia et al., 2008; Ozturk et al., 2002; Pantev et al., 1998; 2001; Schlaug et al., 1995b; Trainor et al., 1999; Watanbe et al., 2007; Wong et al., 2007), although not all of the research supports this (Hutchinson et al., 2003; Keenan et al., 2001).

Length and intensity of musical training may be important. For instance, Schlaug and colleagues (2005) found a significant relationship between amount of practice and degree of change in the corpus callosum, while

Hutchinson and colleagues found that lifetime intensity of practice was correlated to cerebellar volume even though age of commencement was not. Several studies have found a relationship between brain stem encoding of music and speech sounds and years of continuous training and or amount of practice (Musacchia et al., 2007; 2008; Wong et al., 2007).

There may also be gender differences in neurological responses to musical activity. Some research has reported neurological changes only in males (Hutchinson et al., 2003; Lee et al., 2003; Luders et al., 2004), although other research has demonstrated structural neurological change in female musicians (Bermudez et al., 2009; Han et al., 2009). The reasons for these differences need to be established.

Absolute pitch may also be a moderating factor. The development of absolute pitch seems to depend on early music training (Levitin and Rogers, 2005; Zatorre, 2003), although it has also been linked to ongoing musical engagement (Wilson et al., 2012). The structural and functional neurological changes related to absolute pitch and the level at which it operates are distinct from those due to music training (Wilson et al., 2009) presenting possible confounding factors in the assessment of training-induced neuroplasticity.

A further issue relates to individual differences. Several studies have found a subset of participants who have not shown the same degree of improvement in related neuroplasticity in auditory training studies (Gaab et al., 2006; Jancke et al., 2001). Genetic factors may be implicated here (Drayna et al., 2001). Some individuals are known to have difficulty in processing pitch (Cuddy et al., 2005; Peretz et al., 2007). There are also differences in sensitivity to music (Martens et al., 2008; Wengenroth et al., 2010). Learning capacity and the motivation to engage in training may be genetically modulated (for a review see Frank & Fossella, 2011) thereby leading to differences in the outcomes of standardised training (Merrett et al., 2013). This does not mean that pre-existing anatomical factors and behavioural skills cannot be modified by training (Foster & Zatorre, 2010; Golestani et al., 2011). It is also likely that differences in musical experiences prior to formal training play a role in the ongoing impact of training on neuroplasticity (Shahin et al., 2004).

Some of the benefits relating to engagement with music depend on the social aspects of group music making including those relating to:

- motivation and re-engagement with education;
- social cohesion and inclusion;

- pro-social behaviour and team work;
- empathy;
- psychological well-being;
- personal development and self-belief;
- physical development; and
- health.

For these benefits to be realised the quality of the interpersonal interactions between participants and those facilitating the musical activities is crucial. The quality of the teaching, the extent to which individuals experience success, whether engaging with a particular type of music can be integrated with existing self-perceptions, and whether overall it is a positive experience will all contribute to whether there is a positive impact.

Some common characteristics of musical programmes which are beneficial seem to be emerging (Creech et al., 2013). The musical activities themselves need to be highly interactive and enjoyable (Stupar, 2012) and have resonance for the participants. There need to be opportunities for developing new skills and performing; acquiring cultural capital; developing interpersonal bonds and solidarity in pursuing shared goals; ongoing intensity and frequency of contact; developing mutual respect; and recognition and rewards for excellence. Receiving positive affirmation from others relating to musical activities, particularly performance is crucial in enhancing self-beliefs, whatever the age of the participants (e.g. Stupar, 2012; Creech et al., 2014). If the performances are in high status cultural venues this also seems to enhance the impact (Stupar, 2012).

Implications for education

The research undertaken to date exploring the wider benefits of making music suggests that:

- active engagement with making music should start early for the greatest benefits to be realised;
- engagement needs to be sustained over a long period of time to maximise the benefits;
- the activities need to include group work;
- opportunities need to be available for performance;
- the quality of teaching needs to be high;

- the curriculum needs to be broadly based including activities related to pitch and rhythm, singing, instrumental work, composition and improvisation, and the reading of notation;
- to have a positive impact on disaffected and at-risk young people, the musical activities need to be in a genre with which they can relate.

References

Abeles, H. (2007) The effect of string instruction on students' performance on state-mandated achievement tests in mathematics and language arts. Paper presented at the Eastern Division MENC meeting, Hartford CT.

Ahissar, M., Protopapas, A., Reid, M., & Merzenich, M.M. (2000) Auditory processing parallels reading abilities in adults. Proceedings of the National Academy of Sciences, 97, 6832-6837.

Aleman, A., Nieuwenstein, M.R., Böcker, K.B.E. & de Haan , E.H.F. (2000). Music training and mental imagery ability. Neuropsychologia, 38, 1664–1668.

Almau, A. (2005) Music is why we come to school, Improving schools, 8(2), 193-197.

Altenmuller, E.O. (2003). How many music centres are in the brain? In I. Peretz & R. Zatorre (Eds.), The Cognitive Neuroscience of Music (pp 346-356). Oxford: Oxford University Press.

Altenmuller, E.O., Gruhn, W., Parlitz, D. et al. (1997) 'Music learning produces changes in brain activation patterns: a longitudinal DC-EEG-study unit'. International Journal of Arts Medicine, 5, 28-34.

Alvaro, F., Storz A. F., Viti, A., Di Simone, R., Miranda, E., Kirke, A., Badia, T., Helling, G. and Istrate, O. (2010). E-motion Project: Electronic Music & use of ICT for young at risk of exclusion. Final Report of Classroom Testing. Lifelong Learning Programme, Education and Culture DG.Artswork.

Amer, T., Kalender, B., Hasher, L. Trehub, S.E. & Wong, Y. (2013) 'Do older professional musicians have cognitive advantage?' PlOS ONE, 8(8), e 071630 doi/10.1371/journal.pone.0071630

Amunts, K., Schlaug, G., Jäncke, L., Steinmetz, H., Schleicher, A., Dabringhaus, A., et al. (1997). Motor cortex and hand motor skills: structural compliance in the human brain. Human Brain Mapping. 5, 206–215.

Anderson, K. & Overy, K. (2010) Engaging Scottish young offenders in education through music and art, International Journal of Community Music, 3(1), 47-74.

Anshel, A. & Kipper, D.A. (1988). The influence of group singing on trust and cooperation, Journal of Music Therapy, 25(3), 145-155.

Anshel, M. & Marisi, D. (1978). Effect of music and rhythm on physical performance, Research Quarterly, 49, 109-13.

Antrim, D.K. (1945). Do musical talents have higher intelligence? Etude, 63, 127-128.

Anvari S.H., Trainor L.J., Woodside J. & Levy B.Z. (2002). Relations among musical skills, phonological processing, and early reading ability in preschool children. Journal of Experimental Child Psychology, 83, 111-130.

Arnett-Gary, D. (1998). The effects of the arts on academic achievement. Masters Abstracts International, 42(1), 22.

Atterbury, B. (1985). Musical differences in learning-disabled and normal achieving readers, age eight and nine. Psychology of Music, 13(2), 114-123.

Bahna-James, T. (1991). The relationship between mathematics and music: Secondary school perspectives, Journal of Negro Education, 60, 477-485.

Bahr, N., & Christensen, C. (2000). Inter-domain transfer between mathematical skil and musicianship, Journal of Structural Learning and Intelligent Systems, 14, 187-197.

Bailey, B.A. & Davidson, J.W. (2002). Adaptive characteristics of group singing: Perceptions form members of a choir for homeless men, Musicae Scientiae, 6, 221-256.

Bailey, B.A. & Davidson, J. W. (2003). Amateur group singing as a therapeutic agent, Nordic Journal of Music Therapy, 12, 18-32.

Bailey, B.A. & Davidson, J.W. (2005). Effects of group singing and performance for marginalised and middle-class singers, Psychology of Music, 33, 269-303.

Baker, S & Homan, S. (2007). Rap, recidivism and the creative self: A popular music program for young offenders in detention. Journal of Youth Studies, 10(4), 459-476.

Banai, K., Hornickel, J., Skoe, E., Nicol, T., Zecker, S., & Kraus, N. (2009). Reading and subcortical auditory function, Cerebral Cortex, 19(11), 2699-2707.

Bangert, M., Haeusler, U., & Altenmuller, E. (2001). On practice: how the brain connects piano keys and piano sounds, Annals of New York Academy of Sciences, 930, 425-428.

Bangert, M., & Schlaug,G. (2006). Specialization of the special-ized in features of external human brain morphology. European. Journal of Neuroscience. 24, 1832–1834.

Barr, L., Dittmar, M., Roberts, E., & Sheraden, M. (2002). Enhancing student achievement through the improvement of listening skills (ERIC document Reproduction Service No ED465999)

Barwick, J., Valentine, E., West, R. & Wilding, J. (1989). Relations between reading and musical abilities, The British Journal of Educational Psychology, 59, 253-257.

Beck, R., Cesario, T., Yousefi, S. & Enamoto, H. (2000). Choral singing, performance perception and immune system changes in salivary immunoglobulin and cortisol. Music Perception, 18(1), 87-106.

Beck, R.J., Gottfried, T.L., Hall, D.J., Cisler, C.A. & Bozeman, K.W. (2006). Supporting the health of college solo singers: the relationship of positive emotions and stress to changes in the salivary IgA and cortisol during singing. Journal of Learning through the Arts: A research Journal on Arts Integration in Schools and Communities, 2(1), article 19.

Beckham, A.S. (1942). A study of social background and music ability of superior Negro children, Journal of Applied Psychology, 26(2), 210-17.

Beisman, G. (1967). Effect of rhythmic accompaniment upon learning of fundamental motor skills, Research Quarterly, 38, 172-6.

Bengtsson, S.L., Nagy, Z., Skare, S., Forsman, L., Forssberg, H. & Ullen, F. (2005). Extensive piano practicinghas regionally specific effects on white matter development, Nature Neuroscience, 8, 1148-1150.

Bergerson, D., & Motto, E. (2013). Assessing the power of music. Minneapolis: Advocates for Community through Musical Excellence and Breck School's Advanced Mathematics Research.

Bermudez, P., Lerch, J.P., Evans,A.C. & Zatorre, R.J. (2009). Neuroanatomicalcorrelatesof musicianshipasrevealedby corticalthicknessandvoxel- basedmorphometry. Cerebral Cortex 19, 1583–1596.

Besson M., Schon D., Moreno S., Santos A., & Magne C. (2007). Influence of musical expertise and musical training on pitch processing in music and language. Restorative Neurology and Neurosciences, 25, 399–410

Best, J.R., Miller, P.H., Naglieri, J.A. (2011). Relations between Executive Function and Academic Achievement from Ages 5 to 17 in a Large, Representative National Sample. Learning and Individual Differences 21, 327–336.

Bialystok, E., & DePape, A.M. (2009). Music for pain and anxiety in children undergoing medical procedures: a systematic review of randomized controlled trials. Musical expertise, bilingualism, and executive functioning. Journal of Experimental Psychology: Human Perception and Performance, 35, 565-574.

Bidelman, G.M., Gandour, J.T., & Krishnan, A. (2009). Cross domain effects of music and language experience on the representation of pitch in the human auditory brainstem, Journal of Cognitive Neuroscience, 29, 13165-13171.

Bidelman, G.M., Hutka, S., & Moreno, S. (2013). Tone language speakers and musicians share enhanced perceptual and cognitive abilities for musical pitch: Evidence for bidirectionality between the domains of language and music. PLoS ONE, 8(4), e60676 doi:10.1371/journal.pone.0060676

Bidelman, G.M., & Krishnan, A. (2010). Effects of reverberation on brainstem representation of speech in musicians and non-musicians, Brain Research, 1355, 112-125.

Bienstock, S.F. (1942). A predictive study of musical achievement. The pedagogical Seminary and Journal of Genetic Psychology, 61, 135-45.

Bigand, E. & Poulin-Carronnat, B. (2006). Are we 'experienced listeners? A review of the musical capacities that do not depend on formal musical training, Cognition, 100, 100-130.

Bilhartz, T.D, Bruhn, R.A. & Olson, J.E. (1999). The effect of early music training on child cognitive development, Journal of Applied Developmental Psychology, 20, 615-636.

Bittman, B.B., Berk, L.S., Felten, D.L. Westengard, J., Simonton, O.C., Pappas, J. & Ninehouser, M. (2001). Composite effects of group drumming music therapy on modulation of neuroendocrine-immune parameters in normal subjects, Alternative Therapies in Health and Medicine, 7(1), 38-47.

Bittman, B., Dickson, L., & Coddington, K. (2009). Creative musical expression as a catalyst for quality-of-life improvement in inner-city adolescents placed in a court-referred residential treatment program, Advances in Mind-Body Medicine, 24(1), 8-19.

Blakemore, S.J. & Frith, U. (2000). The implications of recent developments in neuroscience for research on teaching and learning. London: Institute of Cognitive Neuroscience.

Bonneville-Roussy, A., Rentfrow., P, Xu, M.K. & Potter, J. (2013). Music through the ages: Trends in musical engagement and preferences from adolescence through middle adulthood, Journal of Personality and Social Psychology, 105(4), 703-717. http://psycnet.apa.org/doi/10.1037/a0033770

Bosacki, S.L. & O'Neill, S.A. (2013). Early adolescents' emotional perceptions and enagement with popular music in everyday life. International Journal of Adolescence and Youth, doi: 10.1080/02673843.2013.785438

Bowles, S.A. (2003). Tune up the mind: The effect of orchestrating music as a reading intervention. Doctoral Dissertation, Indiana University of Pennsylvania, Dissertation Abstracts International, 64(05), 1574A

Bradley, L. & Bryant, P.E (1983). Categorising sounds and learning to read: A causal connection, Nature, 301, 419-421.

Brandler, S., & Rammsayer, T. H. (2003). Differences in mental abilities between musicians and non-musicians. Psychology of Music, 31, 123-138.

Brochard, R. Dufour, A. & Despres, O. (2004). Effect of musical expertise on visuospatial abilities: evidence from reaction times and mental imagery, Brain Cognition, 54, 103-109.

Brodsky W. (1989). Music therapy as an intervention for children with cancer in isolation rooms, Music Therapy, 8, 17-34.

Broh, B.A. (2002). Linking extracurricular programming to academic achievement: who benefits and why? Sociology of Education, 75, 69-95.

Brown, D. (1991). Human Universals. New York: McGraw-Hill

Brown, E.D., Benedett, B & Armistead, M.E. (2010). Arts enrichment and school readiness for children at risk, Early Childhood Research Quarterly, 25, 112-124.

Brown, E.D. & Sax, K.L. (2013). Arts enrichment and preschool emotions for low-income children at risk, Early Childhood Research Quarterly, 28, 337-346.

Brown, J.D. (1980). Identifying problems facing the school band movement. Elkhart: Gemeinhardt Co. Ltd

Brown, J.D. (1985). Strategic marketing for music educators. Elkhart: Gemeinhardt Co. Ltd

Brown, J., Sherrill, C. & Gench, B. (1981). Effects on an integrated physical education/music programme in changing early childhood perceptual-motor performance, Perceptual and Motor Skills, 53(1), 151-4.

Bugaj, K. & Brenner, B. (2011). The effects of music instruction on cognitive development and reading skills: An overview. Bulletin of the Council for Research in Music Education, 189, 89-104.

Bugos, J.A., Perlstein, W.M., McCrae, C.S., Brophy, T.S. & Beden-baugh, P.H. (2007). Individualized piano instruction enhances executive functioning and working memory in older adults. Aging and Mental Health, 11, 464-471.

Burns, D.S., Sledge, R.B., Fuller, L.A., Daggy, J.K., & Monahan, P.O. (2005). Cancer patients' interest and preferences for music therapy. Journal of Music Therapy, 42(3), 185-199.

Burns, S., & Bewick, P. (2011). In Harmony Liverpool: Interim Report Year Two. Royal Liverpool Philharmonic; Department for Education; In Harmony Sistema England.

Burns, S., & Bewick, P. (2012). In Harmony Liverpool - Interim Report: Year Three. Liverpool: In Harmony Liverpool.

Burton, J., Horowitz, R., & Abeles, H. (1999). Learning in and through the arts. In E. Fiske (ed.) Champions of change: The impact of the arts on learning: Curriculum implications. Washington, D.C.: The Arts Education Partnership and The President's Committee on the Arts and the Humanities.

Butkovic, A., Ullen, F. & Mosing, M.A. (2015). Personality related traits as predictors of music practice: Underlying environmental and genetic influences, Personality and Individual Differences, 74, 133-138.

Butzlaff, R. (2000). Can music be used to teach reading? Journal of Aesthetic Education, 34, 167-178.

Byrgen, L.O. Konlaan, B.K. & Johansson, S-E (1996). Attendance at cultural events, reading books or periodicals and making music or singing in a choir as determinants for survival: Swedish interview survey of living conditions, British Medical Journal, 313, 1577-1580.

Cabanac, A., Perlovsky, L., Bonniot-Cabanas, M-C & Cabanac, M. (2013). Music and academic performance, Behaviour Brain Research, 256, 257-260.

Caine, J. (1991). The effects of music on the selected stress behaviours, weight, caloric and formula intake and length of hospital stay of premature and low birth weight neonates in a newborn intensive care unit, Journal of Music Therapy, 28(4), 180-192.

Campe, K., & Kaufman, B. (2013). El Sistema: Development Beyond the Orchestra. Boston, Mass.: El Sistema at Conservatory Lab, Boston, USA.

Caprilli S, Anastasi F, Grotto R, Abeti M, & Messeri A. (2007). Interactive Music as a Treatment for Pain and Stress in Children During Venipuncture: A Randomized Prospective Study, Journal of Developmental Behavioural Pediatrics, 28(5), 399-403.

Cardarelli, D.M. (2003). The effects of music instrumental training on performance on the reading and mathematics portions of the Florida Comprehensive Achievement Test for 3rd grade students. Doctoral Dissertation, University of Central Florida. Dissertation Abstracts International, 64(10), 3624A.

Cassidy, J.W. & Standley, J.M. (1995). The effect of music listening on physiological responses of premature infants in the MCU, Journal of Music Therapy, 32(4), 208-227.

Castañeda-Castañeda, J. C. (2009). Percepción sobre un taller de educación musical, de jóvenes en reclusión en el Marceliano Ossa Lázaro Nicholls 'Créeme'. Universidad Tecnológica de Pereira, Pereira.

Catterall, J.S. (1998). Involvement in the arts and success in secondary school. America for the Arts, 9.

Catterall, J., Chapleau, R. & Iwanga, J. (1999). Involvement in that arts and human development: General involvement and Intensive Involvement in music and theatre arts. In Champions of Change: The impact of the Arts on Learning. Washington DC: Arts Education Partnership.

Catterall J.S. & Rauscher F.H. (2008). Unpacking the impact of music on intelligence. In W. Gruhn & F.H. Rauscher (eds). (pp 171-201). Neurosciences in music pedagogy. Nova Science Publishers, New York.

Chamberlain, J.R. (2003). The relationship between beat competency and reading abilities of third and fifth grade students. Doctoral Dissertation, The University of North Carolina at Greensboro. Dissertation Abstracts International, 64(06), 2016A.

Chan, A & Cheung, M. (1998). Music training improves verbal memory, Nature, 396, 128.

Chan A.S., Ho Y.C. & Cheung M.C. (1998). Music training improves verbal memory, Nature, 396, 128.

Charyton, C. & Snelbecker, G.E. (2007). General, artistic and scientific creativity: attributes of engineering and music students, Creativity Research Journal, 19(2-3), 213-225.

Cheek J.M. & Smith L.R. (1999). Music training and mathematics achievement. Adolescence, 34, 759-761.

Chobert, J., François, C., Velay, J.L.,& Besson, M. (2014). Twelve months of active musical training in 8- to 10-year-old children enhances the preattentive processing of syllabic duration and voice onset time.Cerebral Cortex, 24, 956-967.

Chobert, J., Marie, C., Francois, C., Schon, D., & Besson, M. (2011). Enhanced passive and active processing of syllables in musician children, Journal of Cognitive Neuroscience, 23, 3874-3887.

Choi A-N, Lee, M.S. & Lee, J-S. (2010). Group Music Intervention Reduces Aggression and Improves Self-Esteem in Children with Highly Aggressive Behavior: A Pilot Controlled Trial, Evidence-Based Complementary and Alternative Medicine, 7(2), 213-217.

Clift S. (2012). Singing, wellbeing and health In R. MacDonald, G. Kreutz & L. Mitchell (eds) Music, Health and Wellbeing (pp113-124) Oxford: Oxford University Press.

Clift, S. & Hancox, G. (2001). The perceived benefits of singing: Findings from preliminary surveys of a university college choral society. The Journal of the Royal Society for the Promotion of Health, 121(4), 248-256.

Clift, S., Hancox, G., Staricoff, R. & Whitmore, C. (2008). Singing and Health: A systematic mapping and review of non-clinical research. Sidney de Haan Research Centre for Arts and Health: Canterbury Christ Church University.

Coffman, D.D. & Adamek, M. (1999). The contribution of wind band participation to quality of life of senior adult band members. Dialogue in Instrumental Music Education, 20(1), 25-34.

Cohen, M. A., Evans, K. K., Horowitz, T. S., & Wolfe, J. M. (2011). Auditory and visual memory in musicians and nonmusicians. Psychonomic Bulletin & Review, 18, 586-591.

Cohen, G.D., Perlstein, S., Chapline, J., Kelly, J., Firth, K.M., & Simmens, S. (2006). The impact of professionally conducted cultural programs on the physical health, mental health, and social functioning of older adults. The Gerontologist, 46(6), 726–34.

Cohen, G.D., Perlstein, S., Chapline, J., Kelly, J., Firth, K.M. & Simmens, S. (2007). The impact of professionally conducted cultural programs on the physical health, mental health and social functioning of older adults – 2–year results. Journal of Aging, Humanities and the Arts, 1(1), 5–22.

Conrad, C., Niess, H., Jauch, K.W., Bruns, C.J., Hartl, W., & Welker, L. (2007) 'Overture for growth hormone: requiem for interleukin–6?' Critical Care Medicine, 35(12), 2709–13.

Corrigall, K.A., & Schellenberg, E.G. (2013). Music: The language of emotion. In C. Mohiyeddini, M. Eysenck, & S. Bauer (Eds.) Handbook of psychology of emotions: Recent theoretical perspectives and novel empirical findings (Vol. 2; pp. 299-325). Hauppauge, NY: Nova.

Corrigall, K.A., & Schellenberg, E.G. (in press). Predicting who takes music lessons: Parent and child characteristics. Frontiers in Psychology.

Corrigall, K.A., Schellenberg, E.G., & Misura, N.M. (2013). Music training, cognition, and personality. Frontiers in Psychology, 4: 222. doi: 10.3389/fpsyg.2013.00222

Corrigall, K.A & Trainor, L.J. (2009). Effects of musical training on key and harmony perception, Annals of the New York of Sciences, 1169, 164-168.

Corrigall, K. A., & Trainor, L. J. (2011). Associations between length of music training and reading skills in children. Music Perception, 29, 147-155.

Corriveau, K.H. & Goswami, U. (2009). Rhythmic motor entrainment in children with speech and language impairments: Tapping to the beat, Cortex, 45, 119-130.

Corriveau, K.H. Pasquini, E & Goswami, U. (2007). Basic auditory processing skills and specific language impairment: A new look at an old hypothesis, Journal of Speech, Language and Hearing Research, 50, 647-666.

Costa-Giomi, E. (1999). The effects of three years of piano instruction on children's cognitive development. Journal of Research in Music Education, 47(5), 198-212.

Costa-Giomi, E. (2004). Effects of three years of piano instruction on children's academic achievement, school performance and self-esteem. Psychology of Music, 32, 139-152.

Costa-Giomi, E. (2006) The personality of children who study piano, drop out of piano lessons or never play a note: a longitudinal study. Paper presented at the meeting of the Texas Music Educators Association, February, San Antonia, Texas.

Costa-Giomi, E. (2012). Music instruction and children's intellectual development: the educational context of music participation In R. MacDonald, G. Kreutz, G & L. Mitchell (Eds) Music, health and well-being (pp. 337-355). Oxford: Oxford University Press.

Costa-Giomi, E. & Ryan, C. (2007). The benefits of music instruction: What remains years later. Paper presented at the Symposium for Research in Music Behaviour, March, Baton Rouge, LO.

Courey, S.J.., Balogh, E., Siker, J.R. & Paik, J. (2012). Academic music: music instruction to engage third grade students in learning basic fraction concepts, Educational studies in mathematics, 81(2), 251-278.

Creech, A., Gonzalez-Moreno, P., Lorenzino, L., Waitman, G. et al. (2013) El Sistema and Sistema-Inspired Programmes: A literature review of research, evaluation and critical debates. Sistema Global: San Diego, California.

Creech, A., Hallam, S., Varvarigou & McQueen, H. (2014). Active ageing with music: Supporting well-being in the Third and Fourth ages. London: IOE Press.

Črnčec, A. Wilson, S.J & Prior, M. (2006). The Cognitive and Academic Benefits of Music to Children: Facts and fiction, Educational Psychology: An International Journal of Experimental Educational Psychology, 26(4), 579-594

Cross, I. (2003). Music, cognition, culture and evolution. In I. Peretz and R. Zatorre (Ed) The Cognitive Neuroscience of Music (pp.42-56) Oxford: Oxford University Press

Cross, I. (2009). The evolutionary nature of musical meaning, Musicae Scientae, (special issue on music and evolution), 143-159.

Cross, I. Laurence, F., & Rabinowitch, T-C. (2012). Empathetic creativity in music group practices. In G. McPherson & G. Welch (Eds) The Oxford Handbook of Music Education. (pp 337-353) Oxford: Oxford University Press

Cuddy, L.L., Balkwill, L.L., Peretz, I & Holden, R.R. (2005). Musical difficulties are rare. Annals of the New York Academy of Sciences, 1060(1), 311-324.

Cuesta, J. (2008). Music to my ears: The (many) socioeconomic benefits of music training programmes. Applied Economics Letters, 18(10), 915-918.

Davalos, D.B., Chavez, E.L. & Guardiola (1999). The Effects of Extracurricular Activity, Ethnic Identification, and Perception of School on Student Dropout Rates, Hispanic Journal of Behavioural Sciences, 21(1), 61-73.

Daveson, B.D. (2001). Music therapy and childhood cancer: Goals, methods, patients choice and control during diagnosis, intensive treatment, transplant and palliative care, Music Therapy Perspectives, 19, 114-120.

Davidson, J.W. & Good, J.M.M. (2002). Social and musical co-ordination between members of a string quartet: an exploratory study. Psychology of Music, 30, 186-201.

Davidson, J. & King, E.C. (2004). Strategies for ensemble practice. In A. Williamon (ed.) Musical Excellence. (pp 105-122) Oxford, Oxford University Press.

Daykin, N. Moriarty, Y, Viggiani, N, & Pilkington, P. (2011). Evidence review: Music making with young offenders and young people at risk of offending. Bristol and London: University of West of England/Youth Music.

Deane, K., Hunter, R. & Mullen, P. (2011). Move On Up - an evaluation of Youth Music Mentors. London: Youth Music

De Carbo, N., Fiese, R. & Boyle, D. (1990). A profile of all-state instrumentalists, Research Perspectives in Music Education, 1, 32-40.

De Gratzer, D.P. (1999). Can music help to improve parent child communication: Learning music with parents an Argentine experience, International Journal of Music Education, 34(1), 147-56.

DeLoach Walworth, D. (2005). Procedural-Support Music Therapy in the Healthcare Setting: A Cost–Effectiveness Analysis. Journal of Pediatric Nursing, 20(4), 276-284.

de Roeper, J. & Savelsberg, H.J. (2009). Challenging the youth policy imperative: Engaging young people through the arts. Journal of Youth Studies, 12(2), 209-225.

De Viggiani, N. (2014). A study of young people in the justice system engaged with a creative music programme. Paper presented at the BPS Developmental Section Conference, Amsterdam, September 3rd-5th.

Degé, F., Kubicek, C., & Schwarzer, G. (2011a). Music lessons and intelligence: A relation mediated by executive functions. Music Perception, 29, 195-201.

Degé, F., & Schwarzer, G. (2011). The effect of a music program on phonological awareness in preschoolers. Frontiers in Psychology, 2: 124. doi: 10.3389/fpsyg.2011.00124

Degé, F., Wehrum, S., Stark, R., & Schwarzer, G. (2011b). The influence of two-years school music training in secondary school on visual and auditory memory. European Journal of Developmental Psychology, 8, 608-623.

Degé, F., Wehrum, S., Stark, R., & Schwarzer, G. (2014). Music lessons and academic self-concpep in 12- to 14-year-olds, Musicae Scientiae, 18, 203-215.

Deli, E., Bakle, I. & Zachopoulou, E. (2006). Implementing intervention movement programes for kindergarten children, Journal of Early Childhood Research, 4(1), 5-18.

Derri, V., Tsapakidou, A., Zachopoulou, E. & Kioumourtzoglou, E. (2001). Effect of a music and movement programme on development of locomotor skills by children 4 to 6 years of age, European Journal of Physical Education, 6, 16-25.

Devroop, K. (2009). The effect of instrumental music instruction on disadvantaged South African student's career plans, Musicus, 37(2), 7-12.

Devroop, K. (2012). The social-emotional impact of instrumental music performance on economically disadvantaged South African students, Music Education Research, 14(4), 407-416.

Dezfoolian, L., Zarei, M., Ashayeri, H., & Looyeh, M.Y. (2013). A pilot study on the effects of Orff-based therapeutic music in children with autism spectrum disorder, Music and Medicine, 5, 162-168.

Diamond, A. (1990). The development and neural bases of higher cognitive functions. Introduction. Annals of the New York Academy of Sciences, 608, xiii–lvi. doi: 10.1111/j.1749-6632.1990.tb48888

Diamond, A. (2002). Normal Development of Prefrontal Cortex from Birth to Young Adulthood: Cognitive functions, anatomy, and biochemistry. In D.T Stuss & R.T. Knightly (eds) Principles of Frontal Cortex Funcion, (pp 466-503). New York, NY: Oxford University Press.

Digard, L., Grafin von Sponeck, A. & Liebling, A. (2007). All Together Now: The therapeutic potential of a prison-based music programme, The Prison Service Journal, 170, 3-14.

Dillon, L. (2010). Looked after children and music making: an evidence review. London: Youth Music.

Douglas, S. & Willatts, P. (1994). The relationship between musical ability and literacy skill, Journal of Research in Reading, 17, 99-107.

Dowling, W.J. & Harwood, D. (1986). Music Cognition. New York: Academic Press

Drake, M. (2003) Drum therapy: Exerpt from the book The Shamanic Drum, Retrieved from http:// www.irietones. Com/drumtherapy-article_13. htm

Drayna, D., Manichaikul, A., de Lange, M., Sneider, H., & Spector, T. (2001). Genetic correlates of musical pitch recognition in humans, Science, 291, 1969-1972.

Eastburn, C. (2003). Gongs behind bars: Evaluation report of the Good Vibrations Gamelan in Prisons pilot project. Wellingore: The Firebird Trust.

Eccles, J.S. & Barber, B.L. (1999). Student council, volunteering, bas-ketball, or marching band: What kind of extracurricular in-volvement matters? Journal of Adolescent Research, 14, 10-43.

Eerola, P-S & Eerola, T. (2013). Extended music education enhances the quality of school life, Music Education Research, 16(1), 88-104.

Egaña de Sol, P. (2008). Relevancia e impacto de las actividades ar-tísticas sobre los resultados escolares: El caso de la Orquesta Curanihalue. Unpublished Master's thesis, Universidad de Chile.

Elbert, T., Pantev, C., Wienbruch, C., Rockstroh, B., & Taub, E. (1995). Increased cortical representation of the fingers of the left hand in string players, Science, 270, 305-7.

Elliot, S. & Mikulas, C. (2014). A Study of the Effectiveness of Music Technology Integration on the Development of Language and Literacy Skills. In M. Searson & M. Ochoa (Eds.), Pro-ceedings of Society for Information Technology & Teacher Education International Conference 2014 (pp. 1883-1890). Chesapeake, VA: AACE.

Elmer, S., Meyer, M., & Jäncke, L. (2012). Neurofunctional and behav-ioral correlates of phonetic and temporal categorization in musically trained and untrained subjects. Cerebral Cortex, 22, 650-658.

Elpus, K., & Abril, C.R. (2011). High school music students in the United States: a demographic profile, Journal of Research in Music Education, 59(2), 128-145.

Esqueda Torres, L. (2001). Execution of phase 1 of the monitoring and evaluation plan of the impact of the orchestras national system: Final report. Mérida, Venezuela: Los Andes University, Médicine Faculty, Centre of Psychological Research.

Esqueda Torres, L. (2004). Ejecución de la Fase 3 del Plan de Seguimiento y Evaluación de Impacto del Sistema Nacional de Orquestas de Venezuela: Informe final. Mérida, Venezuela: Centro de Investigaciones Psicológicas - Universidad de Los Andes.

Evaluación de impacto Programa Orquestas Juveniles e Infantiles: Informe de Resultados. (2010). Santiago de Chile: Observatorio Social, Universidad Alberto Hurtado.

Farnsworth, P.R. (1946). Chapter IV: School instruction in music. Review of Educational Research, 16, 182-190.

Faulkner, S., Wood, L., Ivery, P. & Donovan, R. (2012). It is not just music and rhythm... Evaluation of a Drumming-based intervention to improve the social well-being of alienated youth, Children Australia, 37(1), 31-39.

Feldman, A.F. & Matjasko, J.L. (2005). The Role of School-Based Extracurricular Activities in Adolescent Development: A Comprehensive Review and Future Directions, Review of Educational Research, 75(2), 159-210.

Feldman, A.F. & Matjasko, J.L. (2007). Profiles and portfolios of adolescent school-based extracurricular activity participation, Journal of Adolescence, 30(2), 313-32.

Fields, R.D. (2005). Making memories stick, Scientific American, February, 75-81

Fitzpatrick, K.R. (2006). The effect of instrumental music participation and socio-economic status on Ohio fourth- sixth- and ninth- grader profiency test performance, Journal of Research in Music Education, 54, 73-84.

Flohr, J.W., Miller, D.C. & deBeus, R. (2000). EEG studies with young children, Music Educators Journal, 87(2), 28-32.

Forgeard, M., Winner, E., Norton, A., & Schlaug, G. (2008a). Practicing a musical instrument in childhood is associated with enhanced verbal ability and nonverbal reasoning. PLoS One, 3(10): e3566. doi:10.1371/journal.pone.0003566

Foster, N.E.V. & Zatorre, R.J. (2010). Cortical structure predicts success in performing musical transformation judgments. Neuroimage 53, 26–36.

Fracker, G.C. & Howard, V.M. (1928). Correlation between intelligence and musical talent among university students, Psychological Monographs, 39, 157-161.

François, C., Chobert, J., Besson, M., & Schön, D. (2013). Music training and the development of speech segmentation, Cerebral Cortex, 23, 2038-2043.

Franklin, M., Rattray, K., Sledge Moore, K., Moher, J., Chun-Yu, Y., et al. (2008). The effects of musical training on memory, Psychology of Music, 36, 353–365.

Frank, M.J. & Fossella, J.A. (2011). Neurogenetics and pharmacology of learning, motivation,and cogni- tion. Neuropsychopharmacology 36, 133–152.

Fritz, J.B., Elhilali, M. & Shamma, S.A. (2007). Adaptive changes in cortical receptive fields induced by attention to complex sounds, Journal of Neurophysiology, 98(4), 2337-2346.

Froehlich, M.A. (1984). A comparison of the effect of music therapy and medical play therapy on the verbalization behavior of pediatric patients, Journal of Music Therapy, 21(1), 2-15.

Fujioka,T., Ross,B., Kakigi, R., Pantev, C., & Trainor, L.J. (2006). One year of musical training affects development of auditory cortical-evoked fields in young children, Brain, 129, 2593-2608.

Fujioka, T., Trainor, L.J., Ross, B., Kakigi, R. & Pantev, C. (2004). Musical training enhances automatic encoding of melodic contour and interval structure. Journal of Cognitive Neuroscience, 16(6), 1010–1021.

Fukui, H. & Yamashita, M. (2003). The effects of music and visual stress on testosterone and cortisol in men and women. Neuroendocrinology Letters, 24(3/4), 173–80.

Gaab, N, Tallal, P., Lakshminarayanan, K., Archie, J.J., Glover, G.H. & Gabriel, J.D.E (2005). Neural correlates of rapid spectrotemporal processing in musicians and nonmusicians, Annals of the New York Academy of Sciences, 1060, 82-88.

Gaab, N., Gaser, C., & Schlaug, G. (2006).Improvement-related functional plasticity following pitch memory training. Neuroimage, 31, 255. doi:10.1016/j.neuroimage. 2005.11.046

Galarce, E., Berardi, L., & Sanchez, B. (2012). OASIS, OAS Orchestra Programme for Youth at Risk in the Caribbean - Music for Social Change: Final Report: Washington, D.C., Organization of American States.

Gann, E. (2010). The effects of therapeutic hip hop activity groups on perception of self and

social supports in at-risk urban adolescents. PhD Thesis, The Wright Institute, Berkeley, California.

Gardiner, M.E., Fox, A., Knowles, F. & Jeffrey, D. (1996). Learning improved by arts training. Nature, 381 (6580), 284.

Gaser, C., & Schlaug, G. (2003). Brain structures differ between musicians and non-musicians, Journal of Neuroscience, 23, 9240-9245.

Gebel, B., Braun, Ch., Kaza, E., Altenmüller, E. & Lotze, M. (2013). Instrument specific brain activation in sensorimotor and auditory representation in musicians. Neuroimage 74, 37–44.

Gembris, H. (2008). Musical activities in the Third Age: An empirical study with amateur musicians. In A. Daubney, E. Longhi, A. Lamont & D.J. Hargreaves (eds) Musical Development and Learning. Conference proceedings, Second European Conference on Developmental Psychology of Music, Roehampton University, England, 10–12 September, pp 103–08. Hull: G.K. Publishing.

GEN. (2011a). Evaluation of Big Noise, Sistema Scotland. Edinburgh: Scottish Government Social Research.

GEN. (2011b). Evaluation of Big Noise, Sistema Scotland (short version) (No. Research Finding No. 6/2011). Scotland: The Scottish Government: Government Social Research - Arts and Culture.

Geoghegan, N. & Mitchelmore, M. (1996). Possible effects of early childhood music on mathematical achievement, Journal for Australian Research in Early Childhood Education, 1, 57-64.

George, E.M., & Coch, D. (2011). Music training and working memory: An ERP study. Neuropsychologia, 49, 1083-1094.

Charyton, C. & Snelbecker, G.E. (2007). General, Artistic and Scientific Creativity Attributes of Engineering, Creativity Research Journal, 19(2–3), 213–225.

Gibson, C., Folley, B.S., & Park, S. (2009). Enhanced divergent thinking and creativity in musicians: a behavioural and near-infrared spectroscopy study, Brain and Cognition, 69(1), 162-169.

Gillespie, W. & Myors, B. (2000). Personality of rock musicians, Psychology of Music, 28, 154-165.

Golestani, N., Price, C.J. & Scott, S.K. (2011). Born with an ear for dialects? Structural plasticity in the expert phonetician brain. Journal of . Neuroscience, 31, 4213–4220.

Gonsalves, M. (2010). Restoring connection and personal capacities for healing music therapy in Sierra Leone. In M. Elavie Ndura-Ouedraogo, M. Meyer, & J. Atiri (eds) Seeds taking root: Pan-African peace action for the twenty-first century. Lawrenceville, NJ: Africa World Press.

Good, R.H., Gruba, J., & Kaminski, R.A. (2002). Best practices in using dynamic indicators or basic early literacy skills (Dibels) in an outcome-drive model. In A. Thomas & J. Grimes (Eds) Best practices in school psychology (4th Edition), Vol 1, 699-720.

Washington DC: National Association of School Psychologists.

Goodman, E. (2000). Analysing the ensemble in Music Rehearsal and Performance: The Nature and Effects of Interaction in Cello-Piano Duos. Unpublished Doctoral Dissertation, University of London.

Goswami, U., Thomson, J., Richardson, U., Stainthorp, R., Hughes, D., Rosen, S. et al., (2002). Amplitude envelope onsets and developmental dyslexia: A new hypothesis, Proceedings of the National Academy of Sciences, USA, 99, 10911-10916.

Graziano, A.B. Peterson, M., & Shaw, G.L. (1999). Enhanced learning of proportional math through music training and spatial temporal reasoning, Neurological Research, 21, 139-52.

Greasley, A.E., & Lamont, A. (2006). Music preference in adulthood: Why do we like the music we do? In M. Baroni, A.R. Adessi, R. Caterina & M. Costa (Eds) Proceedings of the 9th International Conference on Music Perception and Cognition, (pp 960-966) Bologna, Italy: University of Bologna.

Greasley, A.E. & Lamont, A. (2011). Exploring engagement with music in everyday life using experience sampling methodology, Music Scientiae, 15(1), 45-71.

Gromko, J. (2005). The effect of music instruction on phonemic awareness in beginning readers, Journal of College Reading and Learning, 53(3), 199-209.

Gromko, J., & Poorman, A. (1998). The effect of music training on preschoolers' spatial-temporal task performance. Journal of Research in Music Education, 46, 173-181.

Habibi, A., Ilari, B. Crimi, K., Metke, M., Kaplan, J.T. Joshi, A. Leahy, R.M. et al., (2014). An equal start: absence of group differences in cognitive, social and neural measures prior to music or sports training in children, Frontiers in Human Neuroscience 8, 690, doi 10-3389/fnhum.2014.00690.

Haecker, V., & Ziehen, T. (1922). Zur Vererbung und Entwicklung der musikalischen Begabung. (Inheritance and development of musical talent), Leipzig, J.A. Barth.

Hagen, E., & Bryant, G. (2003). Music and dance as a coalition signalling system, Human Nature, 14, 21-51.

Haimson, J., Swain, D., & Winner, E. (2011a). Are mathematicians more musical than the rest of us? Music Perception, 29, 203-213.

Haimson, J. Swain, D., & Winner, E. (2011b). Do mathematicians have above average musical skill? Music Perception: An interdisciplinary Journal, 29 (2), 203-213.

Haley, J.A. (2001). The relationship between instrumental music instruction and academic achievement in fourth grade students. Doctoral Dissertation, Pace University. Dissertation Abstracts International, 62(09), 2969A.

Hallam, S. (2005). Enhancing learning and motivation through the life span. Institute of Education, University of London

Hallam, S. (2009). Motivation to learn. In S. Hallam, I. Cross & M Thaut (eds) Handbook of Psychology of Music (pp. 285-294) Oxford: Oxford University Press

Hallam, S. (in press). Musical identity, learning and teaching In R. MacDonald, D.J. Hargreaves & D. Miell (eds) Oxford Handbook of Musical Identity. Oxford: Oxford University Press.

Hallam, S., Creech, A., Varvarigou, M., McQueen, H. & Gaunt, H. (2014). Does active engagement in community music support the wellbeing of older people? Arts and Health, 6(2), 101-116.

Hallam, S., & Prince, V. (2000). Research into instrumental music services, London, DfEE.

Hamann, D. Bourassa, R. & Aderman, M. (1990) Creativity and the Arts, Dialogue in Instrumental Music Education, 14, 59-68.

Hamann, D. Bourassa, R. & Aderman, M. (1991). Arts experiences and creativity scores of high school students, Contribution to Music Education, 14, 35-47.

Hampshire, K. R. & Matthijsse, M. (2010). Can arts projects improve young people's wellbeing? A social capital approach, Social Science and Medicine, 71, 708-716.

Han,Y., Yang, H., Lv,Y-T., Zhu, C-Z., He, Y., Tang, H-H. et al. (2009). Gray matter density and white matter integrity in pianists'brain: acombined structural and diffusion tensor MRI study, Neuroscience Leters, 459, 3–6.

Hanna-Pladdy, B., & Gajewski, B. (2012). Recent and past musical activity predicts cognitive aging variability: Direct comparison with general lifestyle activities. Frontiers in Human Neuroscience, 6, 98. doi: 10.3389/fnhum.2012.00198

Hanna-Pladdy, B., & MacKay, A. (2011). The relation between instrumental musical activity and cognitive aging. Neuropsychology, 25, 378-386.

Hannon, E.E. & Trainor, L.J. (2007). Music acquisition: effects of enculturation and formal training on development, Trends in Cognitive Sciences, 11(11), 466-472.

Hansen, M., Wallentin, M., & Vuust, P. (2013). Working memory and musical competence of musicians and non-musicians. Psychology of Music, 41, 779-793.

Hanser, S.B. (2010). Music, health and well-being. In P.N. Juslin & J.A. Sloboda. (Eds) Handbook of music and emotion: Theory, research and applications. Oxford, UK: Oxford University Press.

Harland, J., Kinder, K., Lord, P., Stott, A., Schagen, I., & Haynes, J. (2000). Arts education in secondary schools: Effects and effectiveness. London, NFER/The Arts Council of England, RSA.

Harris, D.A. (2007). Dance/movement therapy approaches to fostering resilience and recovery among African adolescent torture survivors. Torture, 17(2), 134–155.

Harrison, C.S. (1990). Predicting Music Theory Grades: The Relative Efficiency of Academic Ability, Music Experience, and Musical Aptitude, Journal of Research in Music Education, 38(2), 124-137

Hartas, D. (2011). Families' social backgrounds matter: Socio-economic factors, home learning and young children's language, literacy and social outcomes, British Educational Research Journal, 37, 893-914.

Hays, T. & Minichiello, V. (2005). The meaning of music in the lives of older people: A qualitative study, Psychology of Music, 33, 437-451.

Heidenrich, V. (2005). Music therapy in war-effected areas. Intervention, 3(2), 129–134.

Helmbold, N., Rammsayer, T. & Altenmüller, E. (2005). Differences in primary mental abilities between musicians and nonmusicians. Journal of Individual Differences, 26, 74-85.

Hendon, C. & Bohon, L.M. (2008). Hospitalized children's mood differences during play and music therapy, Child Care Health Development, 34(2),141-144.

Henley, J., Caulfield, L.S., Wilson, D. & Wilkinson, D.J. (2012). Good Vibrations: positive change through social music making, Music Education Research, 14(4), 499-520.

Henry, M. & Braucht, M. (2007). Are all-state musicians our future music educators? Southwestern Musician, November, 36-7.

Hesser, B., & Heinemann, H. (eds) (2010). Music as a natural resource: Solutions for social and economic issues. New York, NY, United Nations.

Hetland, L. (2000). Learning to make music enhances spatial reasoning, Journal of Aesthetic Education, 34(3/4), Special Issue, The Arts and Academic Achievement: What the evidence shows (Autumn – Winter, 2000), 179-238.

Hietolahti, A.M. & M. Kalliopuska (1990). Self-esteem and empathy among children actively involved in music, Perceptual and Motor Skills, 71, 1364-6.

Hille, K., Gust, K., Bitz, U., & Kammer, T. (2011). Associations between music education, intelligence, and spelling ability in elementary school, Advances in Cognitive Psychology, 7, 1-6.

Hillier, A., Greher, G., Poto, N. & Dougherty, M. (2012). Positive outcomes following participation in a music intervention for adolescents and young adults on the autistic spectrum, Psychology of Music, 40(2), 201-215.

Hillman, S. (2002). Participatory singing for older people: A perception of benefit, Health Education, 102(4), 163–71.

Hines, S.W. (2000). The effects of motoric and non-motoric music instruction on reading and mathematics achievements of learning disabled students in kindergarten through ninth grade. Doctoral Dissertation, The University of North Carolina at Greensboro, Dissertation Abstracts International, 61(05), 1777A.

Hirt-Mannheimer, J. (1995). Music big for little folks. Teaching Music, 3(2), 38-39.

Ho, Y.C., Cheung, M.C. & Chan, A.S. (2003). Music training improves verbal but not visual memory: Cross sectional and longitudinal explorations in children. Neuropsychology, 17, 439-450.

Hodges, D.A. & O'Connell, D.S. (2007). The impact of music education on academic achievement. In Sounds of Learning Report, NAMM Foundation Sounds of Learning.

Hoffman, D.S. (1995). Relationships between Academic Achievement and Participation in a comprehensive and sequential keyboard-based public school music education programme. Doctoral Dissertation, University of South Carolina. Dissertation Abstracts International, 56(06), 2161A

Hollingworth, L. (1926). Musical sensitivity of children who test above 135 IQ (Standford Binet), Journal of Educational Psychology, 17, 95-105.

Houston D. M., McKee K. J., Carroll L. & Marsh H. (1998). Using humour to promote psychological wellbeing in residential homes for older people, Aging and Mental Health, 2, 328-332.

Hove, M.J. & Risen, J.L. (2009). It's all in the timing: Interpersonal synchrony increases affiliation, Social Cognition, 27(6), 949-960.

Hudziak, J.J., Albaugh, M.D., Duchame, S., Karama, S., Spottswood, M., Crehan, E., Evans, A.C. & Botteron, K.N. (2014). Cortical Thickness Maturation and Duration of Music Training: Health-Promoting Activities Shape Brain Development, Journal of the American Academy of Child & Adolescent Psychiatry, 53(11), 1153-1161.

Humpal, M.E. (1991). The effects of an integrated early childhood music program on soical interaction among children with handicaps and their typical peers, Journal of Music Therapy, 28(3), 161-177.

Humpal, M.E. & Wolf, J. (2007). Music in the Inclusive Classroom, Young Children, 58(2), 103-107.

Hunter, P.G. & Schellenberg, E.G. (2010). Music and emotion. In M.R. Jones, R.R. Fay, & A.N. Popper (eds) Music perception (pp 128-164) New York, NY: Springer,

Huron, D. (2001). Is music an evolutionary adaptation? Annals of the New York Academy of Sciences, 930, 43–61.

Huron, D. (2003). Is music an evolutionary adaptation? In I. Peretz & R. J. Zatorre (Eds.), The cognitive neuroscience of music (pp. 57-75). Oxford, UK: Oxford University Press.

Hurwitz, I., Wolff, P.H., Bortnick, B.D. & Kokas, K. (1975). Nonmusical effects of the Kodaly music curriculum in primary grade children, Journal of Learning Disabilities, 8, 45-52.

Huss, M., Verney, j., Fosker, T., Mead, N & Goswami, U. (2011). Music, rhythm, rise time perception and developmental dyslexia: Perception of musical meter predicts reading and phonology, Cortex, 47, 674-689.

Hutchinson, S., Lee, L.H., Gaab, N., & Schlaug, G. (2003). Cerebellar volume of musicians. Cerebral Cortex, 13, 943-49.

Hyde, K.L., Lerch, J., Norton, A., Forgread, M., Winner, E., Evans, A.C. et al. (2009). Musical training shapes structural brain development, The Journal of Neuroscience, 29(10), 3019-25.

Hyppa, M.T. & Maki, J. (2001). Individual-level relationships between social capital and self-rated health in a bilingual community, Preventative medicine, 32, 148-155.

Israel, E. P. (2012). Instructor perception of El Sistema-based programs in the United States. Unpublished thesis, M Arts (Arts Management), Faculty of the College of the Arts and Sciences, American University, Washington, DC.

Jakobson, L.S., Cuddy, L.L. & Kilgour, A.R. (2003). Time tagging: a key to musicians' superior memory, Music Perception, 20, 307-313.

Jakobson, L., Lewycky, S., Kilgour, A., & Stoesz, B. (2008). Memory for verbal and visual material in highly trained musicians. Music Perception, 26, 41-55.

Jäncke, L., Gaab,N., Wüstenberg, T., Scheich, H. & Heinze, H.J. (2001). Short-term functional plasticity in the human auditory cortex: an fMRIstudy. Brain Research Cognitive Brain Research, 12, 479–485.

Jaschke, A.C., Eggermont, L.H.P., Honing, H. & Scherder, E.J.A. (2013). Music education and its effect on intellectual abilities in children: A systematic review, Reviews in the neurosciences, 24(6), 665-675.

Jellison, J.A., Brooks, B.H. & Huck, A.M. (1984). Structuring Small Groups and Music Reinforcement to Facilitate Positive Interactions and Acceptance of Severely Handicapped Students in the Regular Music Classroom, Journal of Research in Music Education, 32, 243-264.

Jentschke, S. & Koelsch, S. (2009). Musical training modulates the development of syntax processing in children, NeuroImage, 47, 735-744.

Johansson, S.E., Konlaan, B.B. & Bygren, L.O. (2001) Sustaining habits of attending cultural events and maintenance of health: a longitudinal study, Health Promotion International, 16(3), 229-234.

John, O. P., Naumann, L. P., & Soto, C. J. (2008). Paradigm shift to the integrative big-five trait taxonomy: History, measurement, and conceptual Issues. In O. P. John, R. W. Robins, & L. A. Pervin (Eds.), Handbook of personality: Theory and research (pp. 114-158). New York: Guilford.

Johnson, C.M. & Memmott, J.E. (2006) Examination of relationships between music programes of differing quality and standardised test results, Journal of Research in Music Education, 54(4), 293-307.

Johnson, G. & Edelson, J. (2003). Integrating Music and Mathematics in the Elementary Classroom, Teaching children mathematics, 9(8), 474-479

Jones, C., Baker, F., & Day, T. (2004). From healing rituals to music therapy: Bridging the cultural divide between therapist and young Sudanese refugees. The Arts in Psychotherapy, 31(2), 89–100.

Jones, J. L., Lucker, J., Zalewski, C., Brewer, C., & Drayna, D. (2009). Phonological processing in adults with deficits in musical pitch recognition, Journal of Communication Disorders, 42, 226-234.

Jung, R.E. & Haier, R.J. (2007). The parieto-frontal integration theory (P-FIT) of intelligence: Converging neuroimaging evidence, Behavioural and Brain Sciences, 30, 135-154.

Juslin, P.N. & Laukka, P. (2004). Expression, perception and induction of musical emotions: a review and a questionnaire study of everyday listening, Journal of New Music Research, 33(3), 217-238.

Kahn, A.P. (1998). Healthy aging: A study of self-perceptions of well-being. Dissertation abstracts International, 58, 4740B. (UMI No. AAT98-10054)

Kalliopuska, M & Ruokonen, I. (1986). Effects of music-education on development of holistic empathy, Perceptual and Motor Skills, 62, 187-191.

Kalliopuska, M & Ruokonen, I. (1993). A study with follow-up of the effects of music education on holistic development of empathy, Perceptual and Motor Skills, 76, 131-137.

Kalliopuska, M. & Tiitinen, U. (1991). Influence of two developmental programs on the empathy and pro-social behaviour of pre-school-children, Perceptual and Motor Skills, 72, 323-328.

Kalmar, M. (1982). The effets of music education based on Kodaly's directives in nursery school children, Psychology of Music, Special Issue, 63-68.

Kaviani, H., Mirbaha, H., Pournaseh, M., & Sagan, O. (2014). Can music lessons increase the performance of preschool children in IQ tests? Cognitive Processing, 15, 77-84.

Keenan, J.P.,Thangaraj, V.,Halpern, A. R. & Schlaug, G.(2001). Absolute pitch and planum temporale. Neuroimage, 14, 1402–1408.

Keith, D.R., Russell, K. & Weaver, B.S. (2009). The effects of music listening on inconsolable crying in premature infants, Journal of Music Therapy, 46(3), 191-203.

Kemmerer, K.P. (2003) Relationship between the number of hours spent in general music class and reading skills in kindergarten through grade 3. Doctoral Dissertation, Lehigh University. Dissertation Abstracts International, 64(12), 4400A.

Kemp, A E. (1996). The Musical temperament: Psychology and Personality of Musicians. Oxford University Press, Oxford.

Kennedy, J.R. (1998). The effects of musical performance, rational emotive therapy and vicarious experience on the self-efficacy and self-esteem of juvenile delinquents and disadvantaged children. PhD thesis, University of Kansas.

Kenny, A., & Moore, G. (2011). Sing Out With Strings Evaluation Report. Limerick, Ireland: Irish Chamber Orchestra, University of Limerick.

Kiehn, M.T. (2003). Development of Music Creativity among Elementary School Student, Journal of Research in Music Education, 51(4), 278-288.

Kilgour, A.R., Jakobson, L.S., & Cuddy, L.L. (2000). Music training and rate of presentation as mediators of text and song recall. Memory & Cognition, 28, 700-710.

Kim, J., Wigram, T. & Gold, C. (2009). Emotional, motivational and interpersonal responsiveness of children with autism in improvisational music therapy, Autism, 13, 389-409.

Kinney, D.W. (2008). Selected demographic variables, school music participation and achievement test scores of urban middle school students, Journal of Research in Music Education, 56, 145-161.

Kinney, D.W. (2010). Selected nonmusic predictors of urban students' decisions to enrol and persist in middle school band programs, Journal of Research in Music Education, 57, 334-50.

Kirschner, S., & Tomasello, M. (2009). Joint drumming: Social context facilitates synchronization in preschool children, Journal of Experimental Child Psychology, 102(3), 299-314.

Kirschner, S. & Tomasello, M. (2010). Joint music making promotes prosocial behaviour in 4 year old children, Evolution and Human Behaviour, 31(5), 354-364.

Kishon-Rabin, L., Amir, O., Vexler, Y., & Saltz, Y. (2001). Pitch discrimination: Are professional musicians better than non-musicians? Journal of Basic Clinical Physiology and Pharmacology, 12, 125-143.

Klinedinst, R.E. (1991). Predicting Performance Achievement and Retention of Fifth-Grade Instrumental Students, Journal of Research in Music Education, 39(3), 225-238.

Klassen, J. A., Liang, Y., Tjosvold, L., Klassen, T. P., & Hartling, L. (2008). Music for pain and anxiety in children undergoing medical procedures: a systematic review of randomized controlled trials. Ambulatory Pediatrics, 8(2), 117-128.

Koelsch, S., Schroger, E. & Tervaniemi, M. (1999). Superior pre-attentive auditory processing in musicians, NeuroReport, 10, 1309-1313.

Kogan, N. (1997). Reflections on aesthetics and evolution, Critical Review, 11, 193-40.

Kokotsaki, D., & Hallam, S. (2007). Higher Education music students' perceptions of the benefits of participative music making, Music Education Research, 9(1), 93-109.

Kokotsaki, D. & Hallam, S. (2011). The perceived benefits of participative music making for non-music university students: a comparison with music students, Music Education Research, 13(2), 149-172.

Konlaan, B.B., Bygren, L.O. & Johansson, S-E. (2000). Visiting the cinema, concerts, museums or art exhibitions as determinant of survival: a Swedish fourteen-year cohort follow-up study, Scandinavian Journal of Public Health, 28(3), 174-8.

Koutsoupidou, T. & Hargreaves, D. (2009). An experimental study of the effects of improvisation on the development of children's creative thinking in music, Psychology of Music, 37(3), 251-278.

Kraus, N. & Nicol, T. (2014). The cognitive auditory system. In R. Fay & A. Popper (eds) Perspectives on auditory research (pp 299-319) Heidleberg :Springer.

Kraus, N., Slater, J., Thompson, E.C., Hornicked, J., Strait, D.L., Nicol, T & White-Schwoch, T. (2014). Music enrichment programs improve the neural encoding of speech in at-risk children, Journal of Neuroscience, 34(36), 11913-11918.

Kreutz, G., Bongard, S, Rohrmann, S., Grebe, D., Bastian, H.G. & Hodapp, V. (2004). Effects of choir singing or listening on secretory immunoglobulin A, cortisol and emotional state, Journal of Behavioural Medicine, 27(6), 623-635.

Kreutz, G. & Lotze, M. (2008). Neuroscience of music and emotion. In W. Gruhn and R. Rauscher (eds) The Neuroscience of Music Education, (pp 145–69). New York: Nova Publishers.

Krishnan, A., Xu, Y., Gandour, J. & Cariani, P. (2005). Encoding of pitch in the human brainstem is sensitive to language experience, Brain Research: Cognitive Brain Research, 25, 161-168.

Krizman, J. Marian, V., Shook, A., Skoe, E & Kraus, N. (2012). Subcortical encoding of sound is enhanved in bilinguals and relates to executive advantages, Proceedings of the National Academy of Science USA, 109, 7877-7881.

Kubzansky, L.D. (2009). Health and emotion In D. Sander and K.R. Scherer (eds) Oxford companion to emotion and the affective sciences (pp 204–5) Oxford: Oxford University Press.

Kuhn, D. (2002). The effects of active and passive participation in musical activity on the immune system as measured by salivary immunoglobulin A (SigA), Journal of Music Therapy, 39(1), 30-39.

LaGasse, A.B. & Thaut, M.H. (2012). Music and Rehabilitation: Neurological Approaches. In R.MacDonald, Kreutz, G., and Mitchell, L. (eds) Music, health and wellbeing (pp 153–63) Oxford: Oxford University Press.

Lally, E. (2009). The power to heal us with a smile and a song: Senior well–being, music–based participatory arts and the value of qualitative evidence, Journal of Arts and Communities, 1(1), 25–44.

Lamb, S.J. & Gregory, A.H. (1993). The relationship between music and reading in beginning readers, Educational Psychology: An International Journal of Experimental Educational Psychology, 31(1), 19-27.

Lamont, A. (2008). Young children's musical worlds: musical engagement in 3.5-year-olds, Journal of Early Childhood Research, 6(3), 247-261.

Lancashire Learning Skills Council (LLSC) (2003). Evaluation of European Social Fund project, Engaging Disaffected Young People Lancashire County Council.

Lappe, C., Herholtz, S.C., Trainor, L.J. & Pantev, S. (2008). Cortical plasticity induced by short term unimodal and multimodal musical training, Journal of Neuroscience, 28, 9632-9639.

Lashua, B. (2005). Making music, remaking leisure in the Beat of Boyle St. PhD Thesis, Edmonton, University of Alberta.

Lashua, B. & Fox, K. (2007). Defining the Groove: From Remix to Research in the Beat of Boyle Street. Leisure Sciences, 29, 143-158.

Laukka, P. (2007). Uses of music and psychological well-being among the elderly, Journal of Happiness Studies, 8, 215-241.

Le Roux, F.H., Bouic, P.J.D. & Bester, M.M. (2007). The effect of Bach's Magnificat on emotions, immune, and endocrine parameters during physiotherapy treatment of patients with infectious lung conditions, Journal of Music Therapy, 44(2), 156–68.

Lederach, J.P. & Lederach, A.J. (2010). When blood and bones cry out: Journeys through the soundscape of healing and reconciliation. St Lucia, Australia: University of Queensland Press.

Lee, D.J., Chen, Y. & Schlaug, G. (2003). Corpus callosum: musician and gender effects. Neuroreport, 14, 205–209.

Lee, K.M., Skoe, E., Kraus, N. & Ashley, R. (2009). Selective subcortical enhancement of musical intervals in musicians, Journal of Neuroscience, 29, 5832-5840.

Lee, Y-S., Lu, M-J., & Ko, H-P. (2007). Effects of skill training on working memory capacity, Learning and Instruction, 17, 336-344.

Legette, R.M. (1993) The effect of a selected use of music instruction on the self-concept and academic achievement to the musical problem solving abilities of high school students. Doctoral Dissertation, Case Western Reserve University, Dissertation Absracts International. 54(07), 2502A.

Lehmberg, L.J. & Fung, V.C. (2010). Benefits of music participation for senior citizens: A review of the literature, Music Education Research International, 4, 19–30.

Levitin, D.J. & Rogers, S.E. (2005). Absolute pitch: perception, coding, and controversies. Trends in Cognitive Science. 9, 26.

Lewis, K., Demie, F., & Rogers, L. (2011). In Harmony Lambeth: An Evaluation. London: Lambeth Children and Young People's Service with the Institute of Education, University of London.

Lezak, M.D. (ed) (2004). Neuropsychological assessment. Oxford: Oxford University Press.

Li, S., Han,Y., Wang, D., Yang, H., Fan, Y., Lv, Y. et al. (2010). Mapping surface variability of the central sulcus in musicians. Cerebral Cortex, 20, 25–33.

Lichman, S. (2006). Perception and Experience: The Application of Folklore to Coexistence Education in Israeli and Palestinian School-Communities. School of Education Research Seminar Series, Queen's University Belfast, 6 October

Lichman, S. & Sullivan, K. (2000). Harnessing folklore and traditional creativity to promote better understanding between Jewish and Arab children in Israel. In M. Leicester, S. Modgil & C. Modgil (Eds.) Education, Culture and Values, Vol 6. Politics, Education and Citizenship (pp. 66-77). London and Washington, D.C.: The Falmer Press

Lieberman, M.D. (2007). Social cognitive neuro-science: A review of core processes, Annual Review of Psychology, 58, 259-289.

Lillemyr, O.F. (1983). Achievement motivation as a factor in self-perception, Norwegian Research Council for Science and the Humanities, 245-248.

Lindenfelser, K. J., Hense, C., & McFerran, K. (2012). Music Therapy in Pediatric Palliative Care Family-Centered Care to Enhance Quality of Life. American Journal of Hospice and Palliative Medicine, 29(3), 219-226.

Linnakyla, P & Malin, A. (1997). Oppilaiden profiloituminen koulu-viihtyvyyden arvuiubbussa (Student profiles in the light of school engagement. Kasvatus, 28(2), 583-602.

Lipscomb, S.D., Lundell, D., Sevett, C. & Scripp, L. (2008). Rhythm and reading: Improvement of reading fluency using a rhythm based pedagogical technique. Presentation at the 2008 International Conference on Music Perception and Cognition, Japan.

Loewy, J. (2014). First sounds: NICU Rhythm, breath and lullaby research and practice, Paper presented at the conference The Neueosciences and Music – V: Cognitive stimulation and rehabilitation, 29th May to June 1st, Grand Theatre/Palais des Ducs, Dijon.

Long. M. (2014). 'I can read further and there's more meaning while I read': An exploratory study investigating the impact of a rhythm-based music intervention on children's reading, Research Studies in Music Education, 36(1), 107-124.

Longhi, E. & Pickett, N. (2008). Music and well-being in long-term hospitalized children. Psychology of Music, 36, 247-256.

Longhi, E., Pickett, N., & Hargreaves, D. J. (2013). Wellbeing and hospitalized children: Can music help? Psychology of Music.

doi: Published online before print August 22, 2013, doi: 10.1177/0305735613499781

López G., L., & Berríos E., R. (2007). Impacto de las orquestas en la formación de escolares chilenos. Santiago, Chile: Fundación de Orquestas Juveniles e Infatiles de Chile Universidad de Chile.

Lotter, C. B. (2003). Circles of Courage: Music therapy with adolescents in conflict with the law at a community-based setting. M. Mus. thesis, University of Pretoria, South Africa.

Lu, D.T. (1986) The effects of teaching music skills on the development of reading skills among first graders: an experimental study. Doctoral Dissertation, University Washington, Dissertation Abstracts International, 47(12), 4344A.

Luders, E., Gaser, C., Jancke, L. & Schlaug, G. (2004).A voxel-based approach to gray matter asymmetries. Neuroimage, 22, 656–664.

MacDonald, R., Kreutz, G. & Mitchell, L. (2012). Music, health and well-being. New York: Oxford University Press.

Mackenzie, J., & Hamlett, K. (2005). The Music Together Programe: Addressing the needs of 'well' families with young children, Australian Journal of Music Therapy, 16, 43-59.

Magne, C., Schon, D. & Besson, M. (2006). Musician children detect pitch violations in both music and language better than nonmusician children: behavioural and electrophysiological approaches, Journal of Cognitive Neuroscience, 18, 199-211.

Majno, M. (2012). From the model of El Sistema in Venezuela to current applications. Annals of the New York Academy of Sciences, The Neurosciences and Music IV: Learning and Memory (1252).

Malloch, S., Shoemark, H., Cmcec, R., Newnham, C., Paul, C, Prior, M. & Burnham, D. (2012). Music therapy with hospitalised infants – The art and science of communicative musicality, Infant Mental Health Journal, 33, 386-399.

Malloch, S., & Trevarthen, C. (2009). Musicality: Communicating the Vitality and Interests of life. In S. Malloch & C. Trevarthen (Eds.), Communicative Musicality: Exploring the basis of human companionship (Vol. 1, pp. 1–10). Oxford, New York: Oxford University Press.

Malone, A.B. (1996). The effects of live music on the distress of pediatric patients receiving intravenous starts, venipunctures, injections, and heel sticks, Journal of Music Therapy, 33, 19-33.

Marchant-Haycox, S.E. & Wildon, G.D. (1992). Personality and stress in performing artists, Personality and Individual Differences, 13, 1061-1068,

Marie, C., Delogu, F., Lampis, G., Belardinelli, M. O., & Besson, M. (2011a). Influence of musical expertise on segmental and tonal processing in Mandarin Chinese. Journal of Cognitive Neuroscience, 23, 2401-2415.

Marie, C., Magne, C., Besson, M. (2011b). Musicians and the metric structure of words, Journal of Cognitive Neuroscience, 23, 294-305.

Marques, C., Moreno, S., Castro, S.L. & Besson, M. (2007). Musicians detect pitch violation in a foreign language better than non-musicians: Behavioural and electrophysiological evidence, Journal of Cognitive Neuroscience, 19, 1453-1463.

Marsh, C. (2012a). The beat will make you be courage: The role of a secondary school music program in supporting young refugees and newly arrived immigrants in Australia, Research Studies in Music Education, 34(2), 93-111.

Marsh, K. (2012b). Music in the lives of refugee and newly arrived immigrant children in Sydney, Australia. In P. Campbell, & T. Wiggins (Eds.), Oxford handbook of children's musical cultures (pp. 492–509). New York, NY: Oxford University Press.

Marshall, A.T. (1978). An analysis of music curricula an its relationship to the self image of urban black middle school age children: Dissertation Abstracts International, A 38, 6594A-5A

Martens, M.A.,Wilson, S.J. & Reutens, D.C. (2008). Research review: Williams syndrome: a critical review of cognitive, behavioral, and neuro anatomical phenotype. Journal of Child Psychology and Psychiatry, 49, 576–608.

Mathiti, V. (2002). An evaluation of a diversion into music education (DIME) programme for at-risk youth: Implications for programme development. Paper presented at the 14th International congress on Child Abuse and Neglect.

McNeill, W.H. (1995). Keeping together in time: Dance and drill in human history. Cambridge, MA: Harvard University Press.

Mehr, S. A., Schachner, A., Katz, R. C., & Spelke, E. S. (2013). Two randomized trials provide no consistent evidence for nonmusical cognitive benefits of brief preschool music enrichment. PLoS ONE, 8(12): e82007. doi: 10.1371 / journal.pone.0082007

Meinz, E.J. & Hambrick, D.Z. (2010). Deliberate practice is necessary but not sufficient to explain individual differences in piano sight reading skill: The role of working memory capacity, Psychological Science, 21, 914-919.

Merrett, D.L. Peretz, I & Wilson, S.J. (2013). Moderating variables of music training-induced neuroplasticity: a review and discussion. Frontiers of Psychology, 4, 606. doi 10.3389/fpsyg.2013.00606.

Micheyl, C., Delhommeau, K., Perrot, X., & Oxenham, A.J. (2006). Influence of musical and psychoacoustical training on pitch discrimination, Hearing Research, 219, 36-47.

Miendlarzewska, E.A. & Trost, W.J. (2014). How musical training affects cognitive development: rhythm, reward and other modularing variables, Frontiers of Neuroscience, 20(7), 279. doi: 10.3389/fnins.2013.00279

Minguella, M. & Buchanan, C. (2009). The use of music as a tool for social inclusion. Research Report for Cork City Council. Cork: UONER Ltd. Company

Mikenas, E. (2003). Drumming on the edge of leadership: Hand drumming and leadership skills for the new millennium, Percussive Notes, 41(1), 42-45.

Miksza, P. (2007). Music participation and socioeconomic status on correlates of change: a longitudinal analysis of academic achievement, Bulletin of the Council for Research in Music Education, 172, 41-57.

Miksza, P. (2010). Investigating relationships between participation in high school music ensembles and extra-musical outcomes: An analysis of the Education Longitudinal Study of 2002 using bio-ecological development model, Bulletin of the Council for Research in Music Education, 186, 7-25.

Milovanov, R., Huotilainen, M., Välimäki, V., Esquef, P.A.A. & Tervaniemi, M. (2008). Musical aptitude and second language pronunciation skills in school-aged children: Neural and behavioral evidence. Brain Research, 1194, 81-89.

Milovanov, R. & Tervaniemi, M. (2011). The interplay between musical and linguistic aptitudes: A review. Frontiers in Psychology, 2, 321. doi: 10.3389/fpsyg.2011.00321

Miranda, D., & Claes, M. (2009). Music listening, coping, peer affiliation and depression in adolescence, Psychology of Music, 37, 215-233.

Miranda, D. & Gaudreau, P. (2011). Music listening and emotional well-being in adolescence: A person and variable oriented study, European Review of Applied Psychology, 61, 1-11.

Mithen, S. (1996) The Prehistory of the mind. London: Thames and Hudson

Möckel, M., Röcker, L., Störk, T., Vollert, J., Danne, O., Eichstädt, H., Müller, R. & Hochrein, H. (1994). Immediate physiological responses of healthy volunteers to different types of music: cardiovascular, hormonal and mental changes, European Journal of Applied Physiology, 68(6), 451–9.

Montgomery, A.J. (1997). The influence of movement activities on achievement in melodic pitch discrimination and language arts reading readiness skills of selected kindergarten music classes. Doctoral Dissertation, University of Southern Mississippi. Dissertation Abstracts International, 58(09), 3453A.

Moreno, S. & Besson, M. (2006). Musical training and language-related brain electrical activity in children, Psychophysiology, 43, 287-291.

Moreno, S., Bialystok, E., Barac, R., Schellenberg, E. G., Cepeda, N. J., & Chau, T. (2011a). Short-term music training enhances verbal intelligence and executive function, Psychological Science, 22, 1425-1433.

Moreno, S., Friesen, D., & Bialystok, E. (2011b). Effect of music training on promoting preliteracy skills: Preliminary causal evidence, Music Perception, 29, 165-172.

Moreno, S., Marques, C., Santos, A., Santos, M., Castro, S. L., & Besson, M. (2009). Musical training influences linguistic abilities in 8-year-old children: More evidence for brain plasticity. Cerebral Cortex, 19, 712-723.

Moritz, C., Yampolsky, S., Papadelis, G., Thomson, J., & Wolf, M. (2013). Links between early rhythm skills, musical training and phonological awareness, Reading and Writing, 26, 739-769.

Morrison, S.J. (1994). Music students and academic growth. Music Educators Journal, 81(2), 33-36.

Movsesian, E. (1967). The influence of primary teaching music reading skills on the development of basic reading skills in the primary grades. Doctoral Dissertation, University of Southern California. Dissertation Abstracts International, 28(08), 3078A.

Munte, T.F., Nager, W., Beiss, T. Schroeder, C. & Erne, S.N. (2003). Specialization of the Specialised electrophysiological Investigations in Professional Musicians. In G. Avanzini, C. Faienza, D. Minciacchi, L. Lopez, & M.& Majno (Eds) The Neurosciences and Music. (pp. 112-117) New York: New York Academy of Sciences.

Murningham, J.K. & Conlan, D.E. (1991). The dynamics of intense work groups: A study of British string quartets. Administrative Science Quarterly, 36, 165-186.

Musacchia, G., Sams, M., Skoe, E., & Kraus, N. (2007). Musicians have enhanced subcortical auditory and audiovisual processing of speech and music, Proceedings of the National Academy of Sciences of the USA, 104(40), 15894-15898.

Musacchia, G., Strait, D. & Kraus, N. (2008). Relationships between behaviour, brainstem and cortical incoding of seen and heard speech in musicians and nonmusicians, Hearing Research, 241, 34-42.

National Advisory Committee on Creative and Cultural Education (NACCCE) (1999). All our futures: Creativity culture and education. London, Department for Culture, Media and Sport/Department for Education and Employment.

Nelson, A., Hartl, W., Jauch, K–W., Fricchione, G.L., Benson, H., Warshaw, A.L. & Conrad, C. (2008). The impact of music on hypermetabolism in critical illness, Current opinion in Clinical Nutrition and Metabolic Care, 11(6), 790–4.

New Philanthropy Capital (NPC). (2012). The results of NPC's Wellbeing Measure for Music First: National Orchestra for All 2012 Follow Up. London: New Philanthropy Capital.

Nguyen, T. N., Nilsson, S., Hellström, A-L., & Bengtson, A. (2010). Music therapy to reduce pain and anxiety in children with cancer undergoing lumbar puncture: a randomized clinical trial. Journal of Pediatric Oncology Nursing, 27(3), 146-155.

Nicholoson, D. (1972) Music as an aid to learning. Doctoral Dissertation, New York University, Dissertation Abstracts International, 33(01), 0352A.

Nicholson, J.M., Berthelsen, D., Abad, V., Williams, K. & Bradley, J. (2008) Impact of music therapy to promote positive parenting and child development, Journal of Health Psychology, 13, 226-238.

Nicholson, J.M., Berthelsen, D., Williams, K.E. & Abad, V. (2010). National study of an early parenting intervention: Implementation differences on parent and child outcomes: Parenting program implementation, Prevention Science, 11, 360-370.

North, A.C., Hargreaves, D.J., & Hargreaves, J.J. (2004). Use of music in everyday life. Music perception, 22, 41-77.

North, A.C., Hargreaves, D.J. & O'Neill, S.A. (2000) 'The importance of music to adolescents'. British Journal of Educational Psychology, 70, 255-272.

Norton, A., Winner, E., Cronin, K., Overy, K., Lee, D.J. & Schlaug, G. (2005) Are there pre-existing neural, cognitive, or motoric markers for musical ability? Brain and Cognition, 59, 124-134.

Nutley, S.B., Darki, F. & Klingberg, T. (2013). Music practice is associated with development of working memory during childhood and adolescence, Frontiers in Human Neuroscience, 7, 926. doi.org/10.3389%2Ffnhum.2013.00926

O'Callaghan, C., Dun, B., Baron, A., & Barry, P. (2013a). Music's Relevance for Children With Cancer: Music Therapists' Qualitative Clinical Data-Mining Research, Social Work in Health Care, 52(2-3), 125-143.

Odena, O. (2010). Practitioners' views on cross-community music education projects in Northern Ireland: Alienation, socio-economic factors and educational potential, British Educational Research Journal, 36(1), 83-105.

Oechslin, M.S., Van De Ville, D., Laseyras, F., Hauert, C-A., & James, C.E. (2013). Degree of musical expertise modulates higher order brain functioning. Cerebral Cortex, 23, 2213-2224.

Oldfield, A. (2006). Investigation into music therapy for ten pre-school children with autistic spectrum disorder and their parents. In A Oldfield (ed) Interactive music therapy: A positive approach (p 157-188). London, UK: Jessica Kingsley Publishers.

Orsmond, G.I. & Miller, L.K. (1999). Cognitive, musical, and environmental correlates of early music instruction. Psychology of Music, 27, 18-37.

Osborne, N. (2009). Music for children in zones of conflict and post-conflict: A psychobiological approach. In S. Malloch, & C. Trevarthen (Eds.), Communicative musicality: Exploring the basis of human companionship (pp. 331–356). Oxford, UK: Oxford University Press.

Overy, K. (2000). Dyslexia, temporal processing, and music: The potential of music as an early learning aid for dyslexic children. Psychology of Music, 28, 218-229.

Overy, K. (2003). Dyslexia and music: From timing deficits to musical intervention. Annals of the New York Academy of Science, 999, 497-505.

Overy, K (2014). Motor responses to a steady beat. Paper presented at the conference The Neueosciences and Music – V: Cognitive stimulation and rehabilitation, 29th May to June 1st, Grand Theatre/Palais des Ducs, Dijon.

Overy, K., Nicolson, R.I., Fawcett, A.J. & Clarke, E.F. (2003). Dyslexia and music: Measuring musical timing skills, Dyslexia, 9, 18-36.

Öztürk, A.H., Taşçioglu, B., Aktekin, M., Kurtoglu, Z. & Erden, I. (2002). Morphometric comparison of the human corpus callosumin professional musicians and non- musicians by using in vivo magnetic resonance imaging. Journal of Neuroradiology, 29, 29–34.

Painter, G. (1966). The effects of a rhythmic and sensory motor activity program on perceptual motor spatial abilities of kindergarten, Exceptional Children, 33, 113-116.

Pallensen, K.J., Brattico, E., Bailey, C.J., Korvenoja, A., Koivisto, J., Gjedde, A. et al. (2010). Cognitive control in auditory working memory is enhanced in musicians. PloS One 5: e11120. doi: 10.1371/journal.pone.0011120

Pannenborg, H.J. & Pannenborg, W.A. (1915). Die Psycholigie der Musiker (The psychology of musicians), Zeitschrift fur Psychologie, 73, 91-136.

Pantev, C., Oostenveld, R., Engelien, A., Ross, B., Roberts, L.E. & Hoke, M. (1998). Increased audi tory cortical representation in musi cians, Nature 392, 811–814.

Pantev, C., Engelien, A, Candia, V., & Elbert, T. (2001). Representational cortex in musicians. Plastic alterations in response to musical practice, Annals of the New York Academy of Sciences, 930, 300-14.

Pantev, C., Engelien, A., Candia, V. & Elbert, T. (2003) 'Representational cortex in Musicians'. In I. Peretz and R. Zatorre, The Cognitive Neuroscience of Music, (pp. 382-395). Oxford: Oxford University Press

Parbery-Clark, A., Skoe, E., Lam, C., & Kraus, N. (2009). Musician enhancement for speech-in-noise, Ear and Hearing, 30, 653-661.

Parbery-Clark, A., Skoe, E., & Kraus, N. (2009). Musical experience limits the degradative effects of background noise on the neural processing of sound, Journal of Neuroscience, 29, 14100-14107.

Parbery-Clark, A., Strait, D. L., Anderson, S., Hittner, E., & Kraus, N. (2011). Musical experience and the aging auditory system: Implications for cognitive abilities and hearing speech in noise. PLoS ONE,6(5): e18082. doi:10.1371/journal.pone.0018082

Parbery-Clark, A., Tierney, A., Strait, D.L., & Kraus, N. (2012). Musicians have fine-tuned neural distinction of speech syllables, Neuroscience, 219, 111-119.

Parr, S.M. (1985). The effects of graduated exercise at the piano on the pianist's cardiac output, forearm blood flow, heart rate, and blood pressure. Dissertation Abstracts International, 46(6), 1436A. (UMI No. AAT85-18673)

Pascual-Leone, A. (2001). The brain that plays music and is changed by it, Annals of the New York Academy of Sciences, 930, 315-29.

Pasiali, V. (2012). Supporting child-parent interaction: Music therapy as an intervention for promoting mutually responsive orientation, Journal of Music Therapy, 48(3), 303-334.

Patel, A.D. & Daniele, J.R. (2003). An empirical comparison of rhythm in language and music, Cognition, 87, B35-B45.

Patel, A.D. & Iverson, J.R. (2007). The linguistic benefits of musical abilities. Trends in cognitive sciences, 11, 369-372.

Patston, L.L.M. Corballis, M.C, Hogg, S.L. & Tippett, L.J. (2006). The neglect of musicians: Line bisection reveals an opposite bias, Psychological Science, 17, 1029–1031

Patston, L. L., Hogg, S. L., & Tippett, L. J. (2007a). Attention in musicians is more bilateral than in non-musicians. Laterality, 12, 262-272.

Patston, L.M., & Tippett, L.J. (2011). The effect of background music on cognitive performance in musicians and nonmusicians. Music Perception, 29, 173-183.

Pelletier, C.L. (2004). The effect of music on decreasing arousal due to stress: A meta-analysis, Journal of Music Therapy, 41, 192-214.

Peretz, I., Cummings, S. & Dubé, M-P. (2007).The genetics of congenital amusia (ortone-deafness): a family aggregation study. American Journal of Human Genetics, 81, 582–588.

Persellin, D.C. (2000). The effect of activity-based music instruction on spatial-temporal task performance young children, Early Childhood Connections, 6, 21-29.

Pesek, A. (2009). War on the former Yugoslavian territory. Integration of refugee children into the school system and musical activities as an important factor for overcoming war trauma. In B. Clausen, U. Hemetek, & E. Saether (Eds.), Music in motion: Diversity and dialogue in Europe (pp. 359–370). Bielefeld, Germany: Transcript Verlag.

Petrides, K. & Furnham, A. (2001). Trait emotional intelligence: Psychometric investigation with reference to established taxonomies, European Journal of Personality, 15(6), 425-448.

Petrides, K.V., Niven, L., & Mouskounti, T. (2006). The trait emotional intelligence of ballet dancers and musicians, Psicothema, 18, 101-107.

Peynircioğlu, Z., Durgunoğlu, A. & Öney-Küsefoğlu, B. (2002). Phonological awareness and musical aptitude, Journal of Research in Reading, 25(1), 68-80.

Phillips, R.D., Gorton, R.L, Pinciotti, P., & Sachdev, A. (2010). Promising findings on preschoolers' emergent literacy and school readiness in arts-integrated early childhood settings, Early Childhood Education Journal, 38(2), 111-112.

Pietsch, S. & Jansen, P. (2012). Different mental rotation performance in students of music, sport and education, Learning and Individual Differences, 22(1), 159-163.

Pilon, M.A., McIntosh, K.W. & Thaut, M.H. (1998). Auditory versus visual speech timing cues as external rate control to enhance verbal intelligibility in mixed spastic–ataxic dysarthric speakers: A pilot study, Brain Injury,12(9), 793–803.

Piro, J.M. & Ortiz, C. (2009). The effect of piano lessons on the vocabulary and verbal sequencing skills of primary grade students, Psychology of Music, 37(3), 325-347.

Pitts, S,E. (2007). Anything goes: A case study of extra-curricular musical participation in an English secondary school, Music Education Research, 9(1), 145-165.

Portowitz, A. & Klein, P. (2007). MISC Music: A music program to enhance cognitive processing among children with learning difficulties, International Journal of Music Education (Practice), 25, 259-271.

Portowitz, A., Lichtenstein, O., Egorova, L., & Brand, E. (2009). Underlying mechanisms linking music education and cognitive modifiability. Research Studies in Music Education, 31, 107-128.

Preti, C. (2013). Live music as a bridge between hospitals and outside communities: A proposed research framework and a review of the literature. UNESCO Refereed E-Journal, Multi-Disciplinary Research in the Arts, 3(3), 1-18.

Preti, C., & McFerran, K. (2014). Music to promote children's well-being during illness and hospitalization. In G. E. McPherson (Ed.), The Child as Musician. Oxford: Oxford University Press.

Preti, C., & Welch, G. F. (2011). Music in a hospital: The impact of a live music program on pediatric patients and their caregivers. Music and Medicine, 3(4), 213-223.

Putkinen, V., Saarikivi, K., Huotilainen, M., & Tervaniemi, M (2014). Promises of formal and informal musical activities in advancing neurocognitive development throughout childhood. Paper presented at the conference The Neueosciences and Music – V: Cognitive stimulation and rehabilitation, 29th May to June 1st, Grand Theatre/Palais des Ducs, Dijon.

Putkinen, V., Tervaniemi, M. & Huotilainen, M, (2013). Informal musical activities are linked to auditory discrimination and attention in 2–3-year-old children: an event-related potential study, European Journal of Neuroscience, 37(4), 654–661.

QA Research (2012). Young people not in education, employment or training (NEET) and music making. London: Youth Music.

Rabinowitch, T.C., Cross, I & Burnard, P. (2013). Long-term musical group interaction has a positive influence on empathy, Psychology of Music, 41(4), 484-498.

Rabinowitch, T.C., Cross, I & Burnard, P. (2012). Musical group interaction, intersubjectivity and merged subjectivity. In D. Reynolds & M. Reason (Eds) Kinaesthetic Empathy in Creative and Cultural Practices. Bristol: Intellect Press.

Rafferty, K.N. (2003) Will a music and spatial-temporal math program enhance test scores? An analysis of second-grade students' mathematics performance on the Stanford-9 Test and the Capistrano Unified School District CORE level test. Doctoral Dissertation, University of Southern Carolina. Dissertation Abstracts International, 64(12), 4301A.

Rauscher, F.H. (2002). Mozart and the mind: Factual and fictional effects of musical enrichment. In J. Aronson, ed. Improving academic achievement: Impact of psychological factors on education (pp. 269-278). New York: Academic Press

Rauscher, F.H. (2003). Effects of piano, rhythm and singing instruction on the spatial reasoning of at-risk children, In R. Kopiez, A.C. Lehmann, I. Wolther & C. Wolf (eds) Proceedings of the fifth European Society for the Cognitive Sciences of Music, (pp 190-194). Hannover, Germany, Hannover University Press.

Rauscher, F. H. (2005). Musical influences on children's cognitive development. Paper presented at the Royal College of Music, London, UK, October.

Rauscher, F. H. (2009). The impact of music instruction on other skills. In S. Hallam, I. Cross, & M. Thaut (Eds.), The Oxford handbook of music psychology (pp. 244-252). Oxford, UK: Oxford University Press.

Rauscher, F. H., & Hinton, S. C. (2011). Music instruction and its diverse extra-musical benefits. Music Perception, 29, 215-226.

Rauscher, F.H. LeMieux, M & Hinton, S.C. (2005) Selective effects of musc instruction on cognitive performance of at –risk children. Paper presented at the bi-annual meeting of the European Conference on Developmental Psychology. Tenerife, Canary Islands.

Rauscher, F.H., Mosley, J. & Almane, D. (2008) The effects of music instruction on phonemic awareness in kindergarten children. Paper presented at the European Conference on Music Devleopment, Roehampton University, London. UK

Rauscher, F.H., Shaw, G.L. & Ky, K.N. (1995) Listening to Mozart enhances spatial-temporal reasoning: towards a neurophysiological basis, Neuroscience Letters, 185, 44-47.

Rauscher, F.H., Shaw, G.L., Levine, L.J., Wright, E.L., Dennis, W.R. & Newcomb, R. (1997). Music training causes long-term enhancement of preschool children's spatial-temporal reasoning abilities. Neurological Research, 19, 1-8.

Rauscher, F.H. & Zupan, M. (2000). Classroom keyboard instruction improves kindergarten children's spatial-temporal performance: A field experiment. Early Childhood Research Quarterly, 15, 215-228.

Register, D. (2001). The effets of an early intervention music curriculum on prereading/writing, Journal of Music Therapy, 38(3), 239-248.

Register, D. (2004). The effects of live music groups versus an educational children's television program on the emergent literacy of young children, Journal of Music Therapy, 41, 2-27.

Resnicow, J. E., Salovey, P., & Repp, B. H. (2004). Is recognition of emotion in music performance an aspect of emotional intelligence? Music Perception, 22, 145-158.

Revesz, G. (1954) Introduction to the Psychology of Music, University of Oklahoma Press, Norman, Oklahoma

Rickard, N.S., Appelman, P., James, R., Murphy, F., Gill, A. & Bambrick, C. (2013). Orchestrating life skills: The effect of increased school-based music classes on children's social competence and self-esteem, International Journal of Music Education, 31(3), 292-309.

Rickard, N.S., Bambrick, C.J. & Gill, A. (2012). Absence of widespread psychosocial and cognitive affects of school-based music instruction in 10-13 year old students, International Journal of Music Education, 30(1), 57-78.

Rickard, N.S., Vasquez, J.T. Murphy, F., Gill, A. & Toukhsati, S.R. (2010). Benefits of a classroom based music program on verbal memory of primary school children: a longitudinal study, Australian Journal of Music Education, 1, 36-47,

Rickard, N.S. & McFerran, K. (2012). Lifelong engagement with music: Benefits for mental health and wellbeing. New York: Nova Science Publishers, Inc.

Rincón Prat, C. (2013). Promoting personal development through music participation: A case study of youth orchestras in Columbia. In S. O'Neill (Ed.), Personhood and Music Learning. Waterloo, Ontario: Canadian Music Educators Association.

Rinta, T. Purves, R. Welch, G., Stadler Elmer, S & Bissig, R. (2011). Connections between children's feelings of social inclusion and their musical backgrounds, Journal of Social Inclusion 2(2), 35-57.

Robb, S. (2000). The effect of therapeutic music interventions on the behavior of hospitalized children in isolation: Developing contextual support model of music therapy. Journal of Music Therapy, 37(2), 118-146.

Robb S. (2003). Designing music interventions for hospitalized children and adolescents using a contextual support model of music therapy, Music Therapy Perspectives, 21, 27-40.

Roden, I., Grube, D., Bongard, S., & Kreutz, G. (2014a). Does music training enhance working memory performance? Findings from a quasi-experimental longitudinal study. Psychology of Music, 42, 284-298.

Roden, I., Könen, T., Bongard, S., Frankenberg, E., Friedrich, E. K., & Kreutz, G. (2014b). Effects of music training on attention, processing speed and cognitive music abilities—findings from a longitudinal study. Applied Cognitive Psychology. Advance online publication.

Roden, I., Kreutz, G., & Bongard, S. (2012). Effects of a school-based instrumental music programme on verbal and visual memory in primary school children: a longitudinal study. Frontiers in Psychology, 3, 572.

Rodrigues, A. C., Loureiro, M. A., & Caramelli, P. (2013). Long-term musical training may improves different forms of visual attention ability. Brain and Cognition, 82, 229-235.

Roederer, J. (1984). The search for a survival value of music, Music Perception, 1, 350-6.

Ross, V.R. (1936). Relationship between intelligence, scholastic achievement and musical talent, Journal of Juvenile Research, 20, 47-64.

Rudnick, M., Sterritt, G.M. & Flax, M. (1967). Auditory and visual rhythm perception in reading ability, Child Development, 38, 581- 587.

Rusinek, G. (2008). Disaffected learners and school musical culture: an opportunity for inclusion, Research studies in music education, 30(9), 9-23.

Ruthsatz, J., Detterman, D., Griscom, W.S. & Cirullo, B.A. (2008). Becoming an expert in the musical domain: it takes more than just practice, Intelligence, 36, 330-338.

Saarikallio, S. (2006). Differences in adolescents' use of music in mood regulation. In M.Baroni, A.R. Addessor. R. Caterina & M. Costa (eds) Proceedings of the 9th International conference on music perception and cognition. Bologna: Alma Mater Studiorum, University of Bologna.

Saarikallio, S. (2011). Music as emotional self-regulation throughout adulthood, Psychology of Music, 39(3), 307-327.

Saarikallio, S & Erkkila, J. (2007). The role of music in adolescents' mood regulation, Psychology of Music, 35(1), 88-109.

Salomon, G. & Perkins, D.N. (1989). Rocky roads to transfer: rethinking mechanisms of a neglected phenomenon, Educational Psychologist, 24, 113-142.

Salovey, P.M. & Mayer, J.C.D. (2004). Emotional intelligence: Theory, findings and implications, Psychological inquiry, 15(3), 197-215.

Sandgren, M. (2009). Evidence of strong immediate well–being effects of choral singing – with more enjoyment for women than for men. Paper presented at the 7th Triennial Conference of European Society for the Cognitive Sciences of Music (ESCOM 2009), Jyväskylä, Finland. August 12–16.

Savoie, I. (2012). Evaluation Report: Evaluation of Sistema NB: Department of Healthy and Inclusive Communities and Sistema New Brunswick.

Schellenberg, E.G. (2003). Does exposure to music have beneficial side effects? In Peretz, R., and Zatorre, R.J. (eds). The cognitive neuroscience of music (pp 430-448). Nova Science Press, New York.

Schellenberg, E.G. (2004). Music lessons enhance IQ, Psychological Science, 15(8), 511-14.

Schellenberg, E.G. (2005). Music and cognitive abilities, Current directions in Psychological Science, 14, 322-325.

Schellenberg, E. G. (2006). Long-term positive associations between music lessons and IQ, Journal of Educational Psychology, 98, 457-468.

Schellenberg, E. G. (2011a). Examining the association between music lessons and intelligence. British Journal of Psychology, 102, 283-302.

Schellenberg, E. G. (2011b). Music lessons, emotional intelligence, and IQ, Music Perception,29, 185-194.

Schellenberg, E. G. (2014). Music and nonmusical abilities. In G. E. McPherson (Ed.), The child as musician: A handbook of musical development (2nd ed). Oxford, UK: Oxford University Press.

Schellenberg, E. G., & Mankarious, M. (2012). Music training and emotion comprehension in childhood. Emotion, 12, 887-891.

Schellenberg, E.G. & Moreno, S. (2010). Music lessons, pitch processing and g, Psychology of Music, 38(2), 209-221.

Schellenberg, E.G., & Weiss, M.W. (2013). Music and cognitive abilities. In D. Deutsch(Ed.), The Psychology of Music (3rd ed) (pp. 499-550). Amsterdam: Elsevier.

Schlaug, G., Jancke, L., Huang,Y.X., Staiger, J. F. & Steinmetz, H. (1995b). Increased corpus-callosum size in musicians. Neuropsychologia, 33, 1047–1055.

Schlaug, G., Jancke, L., Huang, Y., & Steinmetz, H. (1995a). In vivo evidence of structural brain asummetry in musicians, Science, 267, 699.

Schlaug, G. Norton, A., Overy, K. & Winner, E. (2005). Effects of music training on the child's brain and cognitive development, Annals New York Academy of Science, 1060, 219-230.

Schon, D. (2014). Short and long-term rhythmic interventions in language rehabilitiation Paper presented at the conference The Neueosciences and Music – V: Cognitive stimulation and rehabilitation, 29th May to June 1st, Grand Theatre/Palais des Ducs, Dijon.

Schon, D., Anton, J.L., Roth, M. & Besson, M. (2002). An fMRI study of music sightreading, Neuroreport, 13, 2285-2289.

Schon, D., Magne, C., & Besson, M. (2004). The music of speech: music training facilitates pitch processing in both music and language, Psychophysiology, 41, 341-349.

Schneider, T.W. & Klotz, J. (2000) The impact of music education and athletic participation on academic achievement. ERIC Document Reproduction Service No ED448186.

Schneider, S., Schonle, P.W., Altenmuller, E. & Munte, T.F. (2007). Using musical instruments to improve motor skill recovery following a stroke, Journal of Neurology, 254(10), 1339–46.

Schwartz, K.D. & Fouts, G.T. (2003). Music Preferences, Personality Style, and Developmental Issues of Adolescents, Journal of Youth and Adolescence, 32(3) 205–213.

Sesma, H.M., Mahone, E.M., Levine, T., Eason, S.H. & Cutting, L.E. (2009). The contribution of executive skills to reading comprehension, Child Neuropsychology, 15, 232-246.

Shahin, A., Roberts, L.E., Chau, W., Trainor, L.J. & Miller, L.M. (2008). Music training leads to the development of timbre specific gamma band activity, NeuroImage, 41, 113-122.

Shahin, A., Roberts, L., Pantev, C., Trainor, L., & Ross, B. (2005). Modulation of P2 auditory-evoked responses by the spectral complexity of musical sounds, NeuroReport, 16, 1781-1785.

Shahin, A., Roberts, L.E. & Trainor, L.J. (2004). Enhancement of auditory cortical development by musical experience in children, NeuroReport, 15, 1917-1921.

Shifriss, R., & Bodner, E. (2014). When you're down and troubled: Views on the regulatory power of music, Psychology of Music, Published online before print July 2, 2014, doi: 10.1177/0305735614540360

Shobo, Y. (2001). Arts, Recreation and Children and Arkansas, 2001. ERIC Document Reproduction Service No. ED463076.

Simpson, D.J. (1969). The effect of selected musical studies on growth in general creative potential. Doctoral Dissertation, University of of Southern Calafornia, Dissertation Abstracts 30, 502A-503A.

Slevc, L.R. & Miyake, A. (2006). Individual differences in second language proficiency: does musical ability matter? Psychological Science, 17, 675-681.

Slevin, M., & Slevin, P. (2013). Psychoanalysis and el sistema: Human development through music, International Journal of Applied Psychoanalytic Studies, 10(2), 132–140.

Sloboda, J. A. (1976). Visual perception of musical notation: Registering pitch symbols in memory, Quarterly Journal of Experimental Psychology, 28, 1–16.

Sloboda, J. (1985) The Musical Mind: The Cognitive Psychology of Music. Oxford: Oxford University Press.

Sloboda, J., Lamont, A. & Greasley, A. (2009). Choosing to hear music: motivation process and effect In S. Hallam, I. Cross & M. Thaut (eds) The Oxford Handbook of Music Psychology, (pp. 431-440). Oxford, Oxford University Press

Sluming, V., Barrick, T., Howard, M., Cezayirli, E., Mayes, A. & Roberts, N. (2002). Voxel–based morphometry reveals increased gray matter density in Broca's area in male symphony orchestra musicians. Neuroimage, 17(3), 1613–22.

Sluming, V., Brooks, J., Howard, M., Downes, J. J., & Roberts, N. (2007). Broca's area sup- ports enhanced visuospatial cognition in orchestral musicians, Journal of Neuroscience, 27, 3799-3806.

Smith, J.M. & Szathmary, E. (1995). The major transitions in evolution. Oxford: Oxford University Press.

Smith, R.J. (2001). Boys business: Documenting boys' enagement with music education in two Top End schools. Retrieved from www.octa4.net.au/boysnt/boysmusic.htm on 14-10-14.

Smithurst, S. (2011). In Harmony Norwich Final Pilot Evaluation Report – April 2011. Great Yarmouth, UK: Priory Research Services.

Southgate, D.E., & Roscigno, V.J. (2009). The impact of music on childhood and adolescent achievement, Social Science Quarterly, 90(1), 4-21.

Spintge, R. (2012). Clinical use of music in Operating Theatre'. In R. MacDonald, G. Kreutz & L. Mitchell (eds), Music, Health and Wellbeing (pp. 276–88) Oxford: Oxford University Press.

Spintge, R. & Droh, R. (1992). MusikMedizen – Physiologische Grundlagen und praktische. Anwendungen. Stuttgart: Fischer.

Spychiger, M., Patry, J. Lauper, G., Zimmerman, E., & Weber, E. (1993). Does more music teaching lead to a better social climate. In R. Olechowski & G. Svik (eds) Experimental research in teaching and learning. Bern, Peter Lang.

Stacey, R., Brittain, K. & Kerr, S. (2002). Singing for health: an exploration of the issues, Health Education, 102(4), 156-162.

Standley, J.M. (2008). Does music instruction help children learn to read: Evidence of a meta-analysis. Update: Applications of Research in Music Education, 27, 17-32.

Standley, J.M. & Hughes, J.E. (1997). Evaluation of an early intervention music curriculum for enhancing prereading/writing skills, Music Therapy Perspectives, 15(2), 79-85.

Sterritt, G.M. & Rudnick, M. (1967). Auditory and visual rhythm perception in relation to reading ability in fourth grade boys, Perceptual and Motor Skills, 22, 859-864.

Stewart, L. Henson, R., Kampe, K., Walsh, V., Turner, R., & Frith, U. (2003). Becoming a pianist. An fRMI study of musical literacy acquisition, Annals of the New York Academic Sciences, 999, 204-208.

Stoesz, B., Jakobson, L., Kilgour, A., & Lewycky, S. (2007). Local processing advantage in musicians: Evidence from disembedding and constructional tasks. Music Perception, 25, 153-165.

Strait, D.L., Hornickel, J., & Kraus, N. (2011). Subcortical processing of speech regularities underlies reading and music aptitude in children, Behavioural and brain functions, 7(44) doi 10.1186/1744-9081-7-44.

Strait, D., & Kraus, N. (2011a). Playing music for a smarter ear: Cognitive, perceptual, and neurobiological evidence, Music Perception: An interdisciplinary journal, 29(2), 133-14.

Strait, D.L. & Kraus, N. (2011b). Can you hear me now? Musical training shapes functional brain networks for selective auditory attention and hearing speech in noise, Frontiers of Psychology, 13(2), 113. doi: 10.3389/fpsyg.2011.00113.

Strait, D. & Kraus, N. (2014). Biological impact of auditory expertise across the life-span: musicians as a model of auditory learning, Hearing Research, 308, 109-121.

Strait, D.L., Kraus, N., Parberry-Clark, A. & Ashley, R. (2010). Musical experience shapes top-down auditory mechanisms: evidence from masking and auditory attention performance, Hearing Research, 261, 22-29.

Strait, D., Parbery-Clark, A., Hittner, E., & Kraus, N. (2012). Musical training during early childhood enhances the neural encoding of speech in noise, Brain & Language, 123, 191-201.

Strait, D., Skoe, E., Kraus, N., Ashley, R. (2009a). Musical experience and neural efficiency: Effects of training on subcortical processing of vocal expressions of emotion, European Journal of Neuroscience, 29, 661-668.

Strait, D., Skoe, E., Kraus, N. & Ashley, R. (2009b). Musical experience promotes subcortical efficiency in processing emotional vocal sounds, Annual New York Academic Science: Neurosciences and Music, 1169(1), 209-213.

Stupar, R. (2012). Superar - Chancen für Volksschulkinder durch musikalische Förderung. ARGE Bildungsmanagement Wien, Wien.

Sutton, J. P. (Ed.). (2002). Music, music therapy and trauma. London, UK: Jessica Kingsley.

Sward, R. (1989). Band is a family, Todays Music Educator, Winter, 26-7.

Taetle, L. (1999). The relationship between fine arts participation and daily school attendance at the secondary level, Contributions to Music Education, 26(1), 50-66.

Tallal, P. & Gaab, N. (2006). Dynamic auditory processing, musical experience and language development, Trends in neurosciences, 29, 382-370.

Tallal, P., Miller, S., & Fitch, R.H. (1993). Neurobiological basis of speech: A case for the pre-eminence of temporal processing, Annals of te New York Academy of Sciences, 682, 27-47,

Tarrant, M., North, A.C. & Hargreaves, D.J. (2000). English and American adolescents' reasons for listening to music, Psychology of Music, 28, 166-173.

Tervaniemi, M., Ilvonen, T. Karma, K., Alho, K., & Naatanen, R. (1997). The musical brain: Brain waves reveal the neurophysiological basis of music in human subjects, Neuroscience Letters, 226, 1-4.

Tervaniemi, M., Rytkönen, M., Schröger, E., Ilmoniemi, R.J. & Näätänen, R. (2001).Superior for mation of cortical memory traces for melodic patterns in musicians, Learning and Memory, 8, 295–300

Thaut, M.H., McIntosh, K.H., McIntosh, G.C. & Hoemberg, V. (2001). Auditory rhythmicity enhances movement and speech motor control in patients with Parkinson's disease, Functional Neurology, XVI(2), 163–72.

Thomas, J.M. (2014). To what extent do intervention music classes impact on seven and eight year old children presenting with social, emotional and behavioural difficulties: A study of student learning in a deprived school setting. EdD thesis, University of Bath, Department of Education.

Thomson, J. (2014). Rhythm and literacy abilities: what is the relationship and can rhythm-based interventions help students with dyslexia. Paper presented at the conference The Neurosciences and Music – V: Cognitive stimulation and rehabilitation, 29th May to June 1st, Grand Theatre/Palais des Ducs, Dijon.

Thomson, M. (1993). Teaching the dyslexic child: some evaluation studies. In G. Hales (ed) Meeting Points in Dyslexia: Proceedings of the first International Conference of the British Dyslexia Association.

Thompson, W.F., Schellenberg, E.G. & Husain, G. (2004). Perceiving prosody in speech: Do music lessons help? Emotion, 4, 46-64.

Thompson, W. F., Schellenberg, E. G., & Letnic, A. K. (2012). Fast and loud background music hinders reading comprehension, Psychology of Music, 40, 700-708.

Tierney, A.T. & Kraus, N. (2013). The ability to tap to a beat relates to cognitive, linguistic and perceptual skills, Brain and Language, 124(3), 225-231.

Tomasello, M., Carpenter, M., Call, J., Behne, T. & Moll., H. (2005). Understanding and sharing intentions: the origins of cultural cognition, Behavioural Brain Sciences, 28, 675-691.

Trainor L.J. (2014). The importance of rhythm and interpersonal synchrony in social development, Paper presented at the conference The Neueosciences and Music – V: Cognitive stimulation and rehabilitation, 29th May to June 1st, Grand Theatre/Palais des Ducs, Dijon.

Trainor, L.J., Desjardins, R.N. & Rockel, C. (1999). A comparison of contour and interval process ing in musicians and nonmusicians using event-related potentials. Australian Journal of Psychology. 51, 147–153.

Trainor, L. J., Shahin, A. & Roberts, L.E. (2003). Effects of musical training on the auditory cortex in children, Annals of the New York Academy of Sciences, 999, 506-513.

Travis, F., Harung, H.S. & Lagrosen, Y. (2011). Moral development, executive functioning, peak experiences and brain patterns in professional and amateur classical musicians: Interpreted in light of a Unified Theory of Performance, Conscious Cognition, 20, 1256–1264.

Trehub, S.E. (2014). Singing interventions for managing infant distress. Paper presented at the conference The Neurosciences and Music – V: Cognitive stimulation and rehabilitation, 29th May to June 1st, Grand Theatre/Palais des Ducs, Dijon.

Trent, D.E. (1996). The impact of instrumental education on academic achievement. Doctoral Dissertation, East Texas State University. Dissertation Abstracts International, 57(07), 2933A.

Trimmer, C.G., & Cuddy, L.L. (2008). Emotional intelligence, not music training, predicts recognition of emotional speech prosody, Emotion, 8, 838-849.

Tsang, D.C. & Conrad, N.J. (2011). Music training and reading readiness, Music Perception, 29(2), 157-163.

Tyson, E.H. (2002). Hip Hop Therapy: An Exploratory Study of a Rap Music Intervention with At-Risk and Delinquent Youth, Journal of Poetry Therapy, 15(3), 131-144

Uy, M. (2010). Positive Behavioral and Academic Outcomes in Students Participating in Two After School Music Programs: The Harmony Project and El Sistema. Unpublished manuscript. Berkley's College of Letters and Sciences, University of California.

van Eck, M., Berkhof, H., Nicolson, N. & Sulon, J. (1996). The effects of perceived stress, traits, mood states, and stressful events on salivary cortisol, Psychosomatic Medicine, 58(5), 447–58.

Van Zuijen, T.L. Sussman, E., Winkler, I., Naatanen, R & Tervaniemi, M. (2005). Auditory organisation of sound sequences by a temporal or numerical regularity – A mismatch negativity study comparing musicians and non-musicians, Cognitive Brain Research, 23, 270-276.

Vanderark, S.D., Newman, I., & Bell, S. (1983). The effects of music participation on quality of life in the elderly, Music Therapy, 3, 71-81.

Vastfjall, D. (2002). Emotion induction through music: A review of the musical mood induction procedure, Musicae Scientiae, 6, Special Issue, 171-203.

Vaughn, K. (2000). Music and mathematics: Modest support for the oft-claimed relationship, Journal of Aesthetic Education, 34(3-4), 149-166.

Villalba, M. (2010). La política pública de las orquestas infanto-juveniles. Revista Latinoamericana de Ciencias Sociales, Niñez y Juventud, 8(1), 131-149.

Vohra, S., & Nilsson, S. (2011). Does music therapy reduce pain and anxiety in children with cancer undergoing lumbar puncture? Focus on Alternative and Complementary Therapies, 16(1), 66-67.

Vollert, J.O., Stork, T., Rose, M. & Mockel, M. (2003). Musik als begleitende Therapie bei koronarer Herzkrankheit, Deutsche Medizinische Wochenschrift, 128, 2712–16.

Vuust, P., Gebauer, L., Hansen, N.C., Jorgensen, S.R., Moller, A. & Linnet, J. (2010). Personality influences career choice: sensation seeking in professional musicians, Music Education Research, 12(2), 219-230.

Waaktaar, T., Christie H.J., Inger Helmen Borge, A. & Torgersen, S. (2004). How Can Young People's Resilience be Enhanced? Experiences from a Clinical Intervention Project, Clinical Child Psychology and Psychiatry, 9(2), 167-183.

Wald, G. (2011). Promoción de la salud integral a través del arte con jóvenes en situación de vulnerabilidad social: Estudio comparativo de dos orquestas juveniles de la Ciudad de Buenos

Aires. Eä Revista de Humanidades Médicas & Estudios Sociales de la Ciencia y la Tecnología, 3(1), 1-31.

Wallentin, M., Nielsen, A. H., Friis-Olivarius, M., Vuust, C., & Vuust, P. (2010). The Musical Ear Test, a new reliable test for measuring musical competence, Learning and Individual Differences, 20, 188-196.

Walworth, D.D. (2009). Effects of developmental music groups for parents and premature or typical infants under two years on parental responsiveness and infant social development, Journal of Music Therapy, 46, 32-52.

Watanabe, D., Savion-Lemieux, T. & Penhune, V.B. (2007). The effect of early musical training: evidence for a sensitive period in motor learning, Brain and Cognition, 176, 332–340.

Wechsler, D. (2008). Wechsler Adult Intelligence Scale (4th ed.). San Antonio, TX: Psychological Corporation.

Welch, G.F., Himonides, E., Saunders, J., & Papageorgi, I. (2010). Researching the impact of the national singing programme 'Sing Up' in England: Main findings from the first three years (2007-2010). Children's Singing Development, self-concept and sense of inclusion. International Music Education Research Centre, Institute of Education, University of London.

Welch, G.F., Saunders, J., Hobsbaum, A. & Himonides, E. (2012). Literacy through music: A research evaluation of the New London Orchestra's Literacy through Music Programme. London: International Music Education Research Centre (iMerc), Institute of Education, University of London.

Welch, G.F., Saunders, J., Papageorgi, I., Joyce, H. & Himonides. E. (2009). An instrument for the assessment of children's attitudes to singing, self and social inclusion. London: Institute of Education, University of London

Wengenroth, M., Blatow, M., Heinecke, A., Reinhardt, J., Stippich, C., Hofmann, E., et al. (2013). Increased volume and function of right auditory cortex as a marker for absolute pitch. Cerebral Cortex. doi: 10.1093/cercor/bhs391.[Epub ahead of print].,

Wetter, O. E., Koerner, F., & Schwaninger, A. (2009). Does musical training improve school performance? Instructional Science, 37, 365-374.

White-Schwoch, T., Carr, K.W., Anderson, S, Strait, D.L. & Kraus, N. (2013). Older adults benefit from music training early in life: biological evidence for long term training-driven plasticity, Journal of Neuroscience, 33, 17667-17674.

Whitehead, B.J. (2001). The effect of music-intensive intervention on mathematics scores of middle and high school students. Doctoral Dissertation, Capella University, Dissertation Abstracts International, 62(08), 2710A

Whitehead-Pleaux, A.M., Baryza, M.J., & Sheridan, R.L. (2006). The effects of music therapy on pediatric patients' pain and anxiety during donor site dressing change, Journal of Music Therapy, 43(2), 136-153.

Whitwell, D. (1977) Music learning through performance. Texas: Texas Music Educators Association.

Williams, K.E., Berthelsen, D., Nicholson, J.M., Walker, S. & Abad, V. (2012) The effectiveness of a short-term group music therapy intervention for parents who have a child with a disability, Journal of Music Therapy, 49, 23-44.

Wills, G. & Cooper, C.L. (1988). Pressure Sensitive: Popular Musicians Under Stress. London, Sage.

Wilson, D., Caulfield, L.S. & Atherton. S. (2009). Good vibrations: The long-term impact of a prison based music project, The Prison Service Journal, 182, 27-32.

Wilson, D. & Logan, M. (2006). Breaking down walls - The good vibrations project in prison. Birmingham: Centre for Criminal Justice Policy and Research.

Wilson, D., McKegg, K., Goodwin, D., Black, X., Sauni, P., Toumua, R., et al. (2012). Evaluation of Sistema Aotearoa. Auckland: Institute of Public Policy: An institute of AUT University.

Wilson, S.J., Lusher, D., Martin, C. L., Rayner, G. & McLachlan, N. (2012). Intersecting factors lead to absolute pitch acquisition that is maintained in a "fixed do" environment, Music Perception, 29, 285–296.

Wilson, S.J., Lusher, D., Wan, C.Y., Dudgeon, P. & Reutens, D.C. (2009).The neurocognitive components of pitch process ing: insights from absolute pitch, Cerebral Cortex. 19, 724–732.

Wiltermuth, S. S., & Heath, C. (2009). Synchrony and cooperation, Psychological Science, 20, 1–5.

Winsler, A., Ducenne, L., & Koury, A. (2011). Singing one's way to self-regulation: The role of early music and movement cur- ricula and private speech, Early Education and Develop- ment, 22, 274-304.

Wise, G.W., Hartmann, D.J. & Fisher, B.J. (1992). Exploration of the relationship between choral singing and successful aging, Psychological Reports, 70, 1175-1183.

Wolf, J. (1992). Let's sing it again: Creating music with young children. Young children, 47(2), 56-61.

Wolff, K. (1979). The non-musical outcomes of music education: A review of the literature. Bulletin of the Council for Research in Music Education, 55, 1-27.

Wolff , P.H., Michel, G.F., & Ovrut, M. (1990). The timing of syllable repetitions in developmental dyslexia, Journal of Speech and Hearing Research, 33, 281-289.

Woodward, S.C., Sloth-Neilson, J. & Mathiti, V. (2008). South Africa, the arts and youth in conflict with the law, International Journal of Community Music, 1(1), 69-88.

Wong, P.C.M., Skoe, E., Russo, N.M., Dees, T. & Kraus, N. (2007). Musical experience shapes human brainstorm encoding of linguistic pitch patterns, Nature Neuroscience, 10, 420-422.

Yang, H., Ma, W., Gong, D., Hu, J. & Yao, D. (2014). A longitudinal study on children's music training experience and academic development, Scientific Reports, 4, 5854.

Yoon, J.N. (2000) Music in the classroom: its influence on children's brain development, academic performance, and practical life skills. ERIC Document Reproduction Service No. ED442707.

Young, V.M. & Coleman, A.M. (1979). Some psychological processes in string quartets, Psychology of Music, 7, 12-16.

Zafranas, N. (2004). Piano keyboard training and the spatial-temporal development of young children attending kinder kindergarten classes in Greece, Early Child Development and Care, 17, 199-211.

Zanini, C.R. & Leao, E.T. (2006). Therapeutic choir: A music therapist looks at the new millennium elderly, Voices: A World Forum for Music Therapy, 6(2). Online. normt.uib.no/index.php/voices/article/viewArticle/249/193 (accessed 24 August 2014).

Zatorre, R.J. (2003). Absolute pitch: a model for understanding the influence of genes and development on neural and cognitive function, Nature Neuroscience, 6, 692–695.

Zelazo, P. D. (2004). The development of conscious control in childhood, Trends in Cognitive Sciences, 8, 12-17.

Zendel, B. & Alain, C. (2009). Concurrent sound segregation is enhanced in musicians, Journal of Cognitive Neuroscience, 21, 1488-1498.

Zharinova-Sanderson, O. (2004). Promoting integration and socio-cultural change: Community music therapy with traumatized refugees in Berlin. In M. Pavlicevic & G. Ansdell (eds) Community Music Therapy (pp 233-248). London. Jessica Kingsley.

Zillman, D. & Gan, S. (1997). Musical taste in adolescence. In D.J. Hargreaves & A.C. North The Social Psychology of Music Oxford: Oxford University Press

Zuk, J., Ozernov-Palchik, O., Kim, H., Lakshminarayanan, K., Gabrieli, J.D., Tallal, P. & Gaab, N. (2013). Enhanced syllable discrimination thresholds in musicians, PLoS One, 8, e80546. doi: 10.1371/journal.pone.0080546

Zuk, J., Benjamin, K.A & Gaab, N. (2014). Behavioural and neural correlates of executive functioning in musicians and non-musicians, PLOSone. e99868. doi 10.1371/journalpone.0099868.

Zulauf, M. (1993). Three year experiment in extended music teaching in Switzerland: The different effects observed in a group of

French speaking pupils, Bulletin of the Council for Research in Music Education, 119, 111-21.

Printed in Great Britain
by Amazon.co.uk, Ltd.,
Marston Gate.